LOVEJOY

....

A NOVEL ABOUT DESIRE

DAPHNE SIMPKINS

Quotidian Books

DaphneSimpkins/Quotidian Books

Publisher's Note: This is a work of fiction. Names, characters, places, and incidents are a product of the author's imagination. Locales and public names are sometimes used for atmospheric purposes. Any resemblance to actual people, living or dead, or to businesses, companies, events, institutions, or locales is completely coincidental.

Lovejoy a novel about desire/ Daphne Simpkins 1st edition
ISBN 978-1-7320158-2-1

Contents

"The reality of desire is very different than its reputation."

—Gigi Lovejoy

PART 1

DESIRE

Let him kiss me with the kisses of his mouth!
For your love is better than wine.
The Song of Solomon 1:2

1

LOVE IS A MANY SPLENDORED THING

I was past my prime but not yet old when I met my match, Mr. Lovejoy. The distinguished widower had been part of the background of my community, an old Southern church where tradition is as romantic as the scent of magnolia and the fragrance of the gospel is as abundant as the scent of that flower that ladies in social clubs use for tabletop centerpieces.

Through a natural reluctance to join myself to a ladies' social club that defined me by my gender or marital status, I kept myself apart in the Southern society where God had placed me. I lived on the perimeter where spectators observe and often have opinions. In Sunday school I sat near the wall. In church I sat near the back, where I was occasionally shaken out of my church-time reverie when I heard a man belt out

"Amen" whenever the preacher made a point that might have gone without attention otherwise.

Heads turned at the sound of one of us agreeing out loud with the preacher. Eyes widened to discern the rebel among us-- the man of the Amen. He wasn't hard to spot. The man who vigorously agreed with the preacher was Franklin Lovejoy, a widower of two years.

A handsome man, Mr. Lovejoy sat by himself five pews up from me, and often I watched with amusement the number of ladies who attempted to establish a stronghold beside this older available man. They came and went. I don't know what he said or didn't say that did not encourage the ladies to return. Some did come back, for a while. There were even some Sunday mornings when a single woman nestled in on Lovejoy's left side and another lady snuggled in on his right.

Sunday mornings became like a soap opera to me. I watched, taking note of the women who came and went while the preacher positioned himself behind the pulpit, oblivious to the sexual tensions brewing in the pews.

Most early morning church goers arrive a quarter to the hour in order to get our preferred pews. For that early rising, we not only win our respective cherished pews but are treated to ten minutes of slow-down-and-get-silent-before God music. After the bell chimes announcing the hour, the preacher stands—often shyly. I never like the preacher more than when he first approaches the pulpit with both diffidence and courage, self-protection and openness. A deep silence comes over him just as he is supposed to say a few words about this and that. Then, in the midst of words about love

2

and mercy and beauty and truth that point us toward the God of Wonders, wonder of wonders, Franklin Delmar Lovejoy, a great encourager of deacons, elders, and younger men who try to preach, would release at exactly the moment when the preacher needed a pat on the back, his signature one-word cheer of encouragement, "Amen."

Instantly that single word created a bridge that connected the preacher to all of us. We were one--created to be one in a breath all together. I marveled at the happening, and kept my eye on Mr. Lovejoy, who made it happen.

He was the only one to do it. (There isn't much talking back to the preacher in our church.) I liked the sound of Lovejoy's voice, too. Often when people are described in terms of their attractiveness or appeal the effect of their voice on you is not mentioned, and it should be. The timber of a voice can be very comforting (or surprising); but in Lovejoy's case, his voice was seductive—head-turning. Irresistible. Preachers who wanted to be great preachers coveted Lovejoy's resonant truth-carrying voice and its stirring effect of commanding attention.

Sometimes I whispered the word "Amen" after Mr. Lovejoy just to hear myself speak in church because mostly women don't speak in church, not in the South, anyway; and if you do, it is to cheer or encourage a man in his walk of faith. And so, I was not skilled in speaking and even kept my ideas to myself, believing, rightly I think—amen? —that I simply don't know enough about anything to have a worthwhile opinion.

However, upon whispering "Amen" after Mr. Lovejoy during the church service, I began to learn the sound of my own voice and the power of agreeing and, sometimes, the extraordinary freedom of disagreeing.

No one was more surprised than I after being on a committee called Tender Mercies that I would one day find myself speaking up loudly and with many more words than the man who said, "Amen."   But it was Franklin Delmar Lovejoy who had somehow initiated my freedom of speech.

One amen can cause a ripple effect in others. An amen has the power of contagion.

Mr. Lovejoy had tapped into some kind of unnamed restlessness in me, and his amen had triggered my speaking up in the Tender Mercies meetings. Only my words were not about agreement; they were a loud and serious questioning of perpetuating helplessness in others by helping others too much in the name of Tender Mercies. It is a surprising situation to speak out against giving too much help in the name of mercy in a church where mercy is the sister word for grace. Yet, I without a plan to be one, became that voice of dissent.

My position in the church community changed as a result. It didn't happen the first time I suggested a background check on a stranger who had come in off the street asking for help with his electric bill. I wanted to know if chronically seeking help from neighborhood churches was how he made his living. Later, when one missionary candidate requested plane fare to reach his mission field, I muttered the unpardonable: "That's the place Pat Sajak on "Wheel of Fortune" often sends people as a prize trip when they spell an easy word correctly on the TV game show. I wonder why so many missionaries end up in destinations that are places given away as jackpot prizes on America's game shows."

That's the statement that finally landed me in the dog house outside the perimeter of what is considered good behavior at church. I felt the earth shift under me and heads duck as they calculated how many more months I was scheduled to serve on the Tender Mercies committee before they could finally show me the door. I eyed the door myself, thought about making up a physical condition that I could offer to excuse myself from future committee work; but, in a fit of menopausal madness I spoke to God while looking at myself in the mirror, "What's sinful about having an unpopular opinion?" So, I stayed—mainly to find out what, if anything, would be done about the problem—me.

I walked the widening fault line created by my questions, growing increasingly apart and alone as others who knew of my meddlesome troublemaking began to turn gently to the side when I passed by. You don't have to be formally rebuked at church, put in time out by the elders, or receive a formal letter of warning that you are in danger of excommunication to know you are on the outs with church leadership. The more powerful event at church is to be very quietly and effectively shunned. Most people leave a church of their own accord as an effect of shunning, sheepishly disappearing into the future with nary a backward glance. But I lived in the neighborhood, and I didn't want to find another church far enough away so that my reputation would not precede me or close enough that people who knew me here would know me there and know about me. So, I stayed in my pew, whispering "Amen" after Mr. Lovejoy, and keeping my eye on the calendar to count down the days of my impending expiration on the Tender Mercies committee. People do forget, over time. After a while they would forget my trespasses, and in the forgetting, forgive?

That hopeful plan did not stop me from continuing to speak and question spending decisions in committee meetings, however. No matter how many times I gave myself a talking to about being quiet and more agreeable, in the very next meeting someone would paint a scenario that required mercy, an expensive hand out to someone in a sports ministry or to a cowboy on the rodeo circuit who wanted to tell people about the Lawd in between bronco bustin'. That night, I said, "Tell that good ole cowboy if he's not a good enough bronco buster to win the rodeo prize money and support himself with his chosen vocation, maybe he should open a lawn service. Like the Apostle Paul, you can make tents and earn a living cutting yards while you tell homeowners about the Lawd."

I've been witnessed to by a number of lawn mower men, coffee-serving waitresses, and hair-cutting artistes. You can do all kinds of work, testify to the good news that salvation is through faith alone in Jesus, and not take money from the church to say those words wherever you go.

It was a long meeting with lots of sighin'. I ended up sitting by myself at the end of the long conference table, and I understood why. The implications of saying no to people needing tender mercies were not hard to understand. If we stopped giving out the money then the Tender Mercies committee and the person in charge of the committee was out of a job. Then there would be no stories to tell to elicit more contributions from the congregation to give to people who needed money, and down the road after a while, eventually, surely, the gospel.

That was a sticking point, you see. I kept saying, "Tell 'em about Jesus, and then tell them to get a job. After that, teach that working man to tithe and let the Lord show him how to become a good steward of himself, including the gift of labor. Work is a gift. In so many ways, a hand-out is not the gift we think it is."

In the year of the 500th anniversary of the Reformation, out of the blue and on a low humidity morning when my freshly trimmed hair with newly added streaks of blonde and a saucy little flip of a curl on the left side of my bangs that "Gives your face a lift, Miss Cindy, so please don't try to iron it out," said my hair dresser, Mr. Lovejoy of the 'Amen' asked me to lunch.

But first, he extricated himself from the presence of a woman I greatly admire who was well groomed, wore taupe tummy control panty hose without gasping for air, could walk in black patent leather high heels without teetering, had thick brown lustrous Grand Ole Opry hair that was immune to humidity, could make small talk better than Paula Deen, and her laugh was a light tinkling sound that made you think of Christmas bells. Mr. Lovejoy excused himself from the lady with the tinkling Christmas bells laugh and asked me—the church leper-- to Sunday lunch.

Thinking that it was about time someone delivered the criticism from above formally that my opinions were proving problematic, I lit up girlishly, automatically, and said, sweetly, with a honeyed smile on my face, "Oh, thank you so much" to his invitation to Sunday lunch in order to get this problem of being rebuked by the leadership behind me. *Go ahead, Mr. Lovejoy. Tell me how wrong I am and that I have been excused from further service on the committee, and I will turn the other cheek and disappear like the vapor I am.* And in that moment of planning my reply to what he would surely say during lunch, I wondered if much of what I had been saying on the committee was perversely spoken to get myself kicked off the committee so that I didn't have to formally quit.

I hate quitters and deep down I didn't want to be one.

2

DON'T BLAME ME

M r. Lovejoy waited for me by the church's side door that led to the street where his car was parked. Holding the heavy wooden door open for me to pass through, he said, his voice more a whisper than a command, "My car is right over there. Country Club okay with you?"

I thought the offer of lunch at the Country Club was unnecessarily generous for a man with the delegated, and I was sure, highly discreet mission to excuse me ever so politely from future church service on the Tender Mercies committee. Elder Lovejoy could have gotten by cheaper and accomplished his task with a standard meat-and-three vegetable lunch at any of the local restaurants where 8.99 was the price of Sunday lunch if you didn't order iced tea.

I routinely drink water with Sunday lunch to save the two dollars for a glass of tea because these small spending decisions that result in savings are how I accumulate enough money to contribute to the Tender Mercies fund. When I don't drink iced tea on Sunday that saved two dollars goes toward missions support, and it matters. I like iced tea. It is my favorite drink; and when I don't drink iced tea, it is my drink offering unto the Lord, a sacrifice in the name of tender mercy. (The church likes to call that kind of giving by other names, but I like to use my own labels!)

A half foot taller than I, Mr. Lovejoy walked silently beside me, careful to have his arm ready for me to hold onto if I needed help balancing on the concrete steps that led to the street where he was parked. In that short walk from the church to his car I was suddenly aware of the fragrance of magnolia. Suddenly I was flooded with the aroma, as if a breeze had wafted through the neighborhood and carried the scent from every tree nearby right to us. When we reached his car, a twelve-year old Buick of hard body and a trusty navy blue, Mr. Lovejoy opened the door for me and waited for me to sit down and swing my legs in and situate them. I have never been very good at being tended to by a man this way, having spent most of my life climbing in and out of cars alone and getting onto and out of chairs without any kind of masculine assistance.

The last time a man helped me with my chair was at the Tender Mercies committee meeting four months ago. Surprised by Dick's sudden help with sitting down, I twisted my foot under the chair, and it had gotten wedged sideways with my ankle straining and my foot bent and turned toward the floor. It took me through the opening prayer and the reading of the minutes from the previous meeting before I could get my foot unstuck. And then my ankle throbbed, and it didn't stop hurting. Upon rising an hour later, I pretended my discomfort was from a leg that had gone asleep, but that wasn't true. I got my foot stuck under the chair when Dick, the man helping me onto and later out of the chair, surprised me both times with his gallantry.

Settling into Mr. Lovejoy's car, I felt a remembered fear of getting hurt and a kind of test being taken about what it means to be a woman with a man, and I didn't know whether or not I was going to fail: I was sure I would.

Lovejoy was not impatient. He let me settle inside the car on the passenger side and arrange my three-year old black leather purse at my feet. Relaxed and patient, he leaned forward smiling, his breath a surprising fragrance of mint and vanilla—what kind of mouth wash is minty vanilla? --smiled at me, warmly, and his eyes, the color of the old South, blue-grey twinkled with amusement. For the strangest second in my life (at that time) I thought Mr. Lovejoy fought the urge to lean in and kiss me. It felt like that, really.

The door closed upon this suspicion of desire, and Mr. Lovejoy walked around the back of the car to reach the driver's side. I was suddenly aware in ways that I had never really waked up to before that I was a woman; and when Mr. Lovejoy positioned himself behind the steering wheel, I saw him not as an attractive elder in my hometown church who was well fixed, well respected, and desired by most of the older single women and lonely widows in the congregation, but as someone much more dangerous. Franklin Lovejoy was a man with a membership at the Country Club who attended to a woman as if she were a lady, and he was about to buy me lunch. I was sure the ax would ultimately fall and I would soon find myself separated from the Tender Mercies committee; but until it did, I felt weak and kind of excited too. It was a strange feeling, and once I got over being afraid of what Mr. Lovejoy would do next, I liked feeling that way.

He drove us the short distance to the Country Club, steering, leading, guiding in ways that made me feel protected and something I hadn't known in a long time and which I did not expect to feel when I early on believed he was going to shepherd me into a more graceful and ladylike silence at church. I felt the most intoxicating sensation of being safe. If danger came, I believed Mr. Lovejoy would stand between me and whatever the danger was. When a man can make you feel safe, he becomes, paradoxically and ironically too, very dangerous. Even the strongest woman becomes weak with a man like that.

Walking up the steps to the Country Club, I began to experience the forgotten feeling of being intoxicatingly and dangerously safe, and when Mr. Lovejoy opened the door for me, I stepped out of the noontime sunlight and into the shadows of the Club's well-appointed lobby. Almost instantly, I was not only safe in his company, I felt at home with him too. We went from being polite acquaintances to something more just by crossing a common threshold. A friendly rapport settled upon us. We became instantly easy with one another. And I became more curious about him.

Having watched the soap opera called Lovejoy's way with the ladies on Sunday morning from five pews behind, I knew what the back of his head looked like. In the car, I had checked out his profile. He had a nicely shaped head. In the Country Club dining room sitting cross from him at the table I beamed at him in my most friendly way while taking an inventory of his features. His eyes crinkled with good humor; his smile was paradoxically quick and lazy. His hands were gentle and controlled. He was comfortable in his skin. At ease, he draped his thick white cloth napkin across his knees, and I immediately did the same thing. He wasn't wearing a wedding band.

Three people attended us: the man who escorted us to the table, the lady who brought the basket of warm breads, and Alfred the waiter who announced that he "Would be taking care of us."

Just as I was going to wave away the offer of iced tea and request my usual frugal glass of water, Lovejoy raised one of his musical hands—yes, like a conductor's, he could lead music with those hands-- and he ordered a mimosa for us each, an unexpected treat. Looking up at Alfred, Lovejoy said without asking me if I agreed, "The lady and I will not be in a hurry today. We are getting to know one another."

Lovejoy's voice was warm and laced with amusement and entreaty to the server: *Be on our side, won't you?*

"Understood, sir," Alfred replied, bowing slightly, and he smiled first at him and then winked at me, an impertinence I wouldn't have understood if Mr. Lovejoy hadn't leaned toward me slightly just as the golfers outside on the Country Club golf course moved out toward the first hole and said, "Alfred understands what you do not yet realize." Lovejoy took a measured sip of the ice water already on the table before setting the glass back down. Holding my gaze, he said easily, "I want you."

I waited and then finally asked, "Want me to do what?"

He stifled an amused chuckle and blotted his lips with the white cotton napkin, taking his time amending his statement. "I mean that I want to court you."

The second statement was no less surprising than the first. And what did he expect me to say or do? I took a nervous sip of ice water and choked. Coughing bought me some time to think, but it didn't do any good. I couldn't think of anything to say, which was apparently okay with him.

His gaze held mine. I didn't blink either, having grown up in the South where we typically for fun try to stare someone else down. We can also for just a little while read someone else's mind that way. Holding his gaze, I saw that Mr. Lovejoy wasn't asking my permission. He was stating his plan. His blue grey eyes were rich and warm and amused by my surprise.

Immediately, I dropped my gaze and saw the sleeve of his blue striped seersucker suit moving dangerously close to the small saucer of butter rosettes, 'Little boutonnieres of butter,' I thought, and I would have tried to say something to warn him about the butter just about to get on his sleeve, but the mimosas arrived, icy orange juice frothy with chilled champagne. I don't like a mimosa more than iced tea, but I do like mimosas. Lovejoy signaled gratitude to Alfred who had brought them. Then he lifted his glass toward me, and I, a long-time imitator of others and trained in the South to be responsive and polite, lifted my glass too.

Lovejoy touched the base of his flute to mine. When I allowed that, it felt to him—and to me, too—as if I had in my silent way as I did at church, mumbled "Amen" to his announcement that he wanted to court me, and my first sip of the frothy aperitif was a polite assent to his plan.

His words bubbled inside of me.

The words "court you" were as old-fashioned as he was, and while I sipped my mimosa, I wondered exactly what he had meant. I concluded that I didn't know. Date? Keep company with? Sit next to in church? What exactly did "court you" mean?

Elder Franklin Lovejoy was in no hurry to elaborate. We ate slowly as if he hadn't said anything at all. The food was remarkably good. We were served small green salads with hearts of palm, candied pecans, sunflower seeds, all spritzed (doused is too strong a verb for how little dressing was used) in a raspberry vinaigrette. Next, Alfred brought us sautéed shrimp and steaming buttery grits. I have always hated shrimp and grits, (Those two things are too pale to go together!), but these were rather tasty.

Then, Lovejoy insisted I try the bread pudding with whiskey sauce. "It's more of a souffle than a dense heavy bread pudding that you might be expecting," he promised. "New Orleans could be inspired by this chef's recipe for bread pudding."

I didn't say no to the bread pudding.

Alfred brought it from the dessert table, and placed two steaming bowls in front of us. I could smell the whiskey. Lovejoy inhaled and grinned. He waited for me to spoon the first bite. I did. The warm whiskey sauce dribbled down my chin. Lovejoy leaned over and daubed my face with his own thick cloth napkin. The quick intimacy of his action embarrassed me.

"Puddin' looks good on you," he assured me. His voice was laced with hidden meanings, and his eyes teased me to laugh at myself. I was able to smile, but just barely.

I applied myself to finishing the dessert, not looking up until I had eaten it all. When I finally did sit back to face him, Lovejoy smiled broadly, "I like a woman who really eats on a date instead of just toying with her food."

We were on a date! Until he said those words, I did not know that.

"I love to eat," I replied with enthusiasm.

"One of the great pleasures in life," he replied. "But there are others that I would like to share with you." His eyes dared me to be curious.

I smiled tremulously, cautiously, taking deep breaths and wondering if I should grab my purse and make a run for the front door. Sensing my desire to escape the dangerous safety he offered, Lovejoy suggested a drive in the country. Before I could say, 'I usually take a nap on Sunday afternoon,' he finessed the bill, and quietly escorted me back to his car, which he had parked in the shade.

We exited the Country Club's parking lot onto a city road that soon becomes a country lane, heading left instead of right. Five miles later we were still going south.

"I've a good mind to take you to the beach and give you supper at dusk at the Grand Hotel, but I suspect we would both be kicked out of the church for that detour." He looked at me archly, his oceanic eyes twinkling mischief.

Lovejoy

"Have you been to The Grand and seen the sun set over the water? It falls fast, a red ball in the sky, sitting at the horizon until it disappears. But before then, you can be a part of the water, the sky, know the motion of the fish and the flight of birds that are fishing the waters and see in the distance the City of Mobile and beyond. You can see the whole world from there if you know how to look for it," Lovejoy promised me, and then I looked into his eyes and saw it all right then in his eyes just as he described it.

My mouth went dry, and I scooted over and hugged the passenger door. I had never met a man who had the whole world in his eyes and knew just what he wanted. No one had ever wanted me like this before and certainly not a man who could have his pick of the ladies at church.

He kept talking. "I would like to take you there on our honeymoon after I have courted you a while and after you have learned to trust me. That will happen," Lovejoy prophesied with conviction. His hands were easy on the steering wheel, and I wondered if he had ever trained horses or sailed boats that required bridles, cords, and ropes being pulled and adjusted.

He did not look at me when he said those words, but I studied him. His face was friendly with shadows and light. Once upon a time I had studied art in college; and in that instant, I wanted to draw him. Yes, I wanted to capture Lovejoy's likeness in my hands. I hadn't drawn anyone in years, and I felt my hand itch to hold a pencil and catch his likeness. I drummed the top of my thigh instead, and he asked me without looking over, "Are you nervous about something?"

I could only shake my head in reply, and though he did not look at me directly I felt that he understood something true about the drumming of my fingers and what they actually meant. It would take me almost five years to understand that wanting to draw Lovejoy was actually the beginning of my desire for him. But then, in that first excursion, I only thought of drawing as a reflex, an impulse, some echo from my youth when I was a girl who had liked to draw and believed in her innocence that a future should accommodate the report of beauty's presence created in art.

Strangely, my thrumming fingers started a rhythm that triggered music in him.

He began to hum an old song that I hadn't heard in years. I think it was an old Perry Como song. Later, I would pay attention to the songs that Lovejoy hummed absentmindedly, as a way, I thought, to figuring out what he was secretly thinking, but I didn't know that then. I just thought he sounded happy. I recalled that I liked Perry Como's voice and music, and I tried to let my legs relax because I couldn't cross them in the car. I wanted my legs to behave themselves and rest in a ladylike position, ankles crossed, black polyester skirt tucked modestly over my knees. Through will alone, I made my hands be still in my lap, but it was hard.

I was wrestling with self-consciousness when Mr. Lovejoy steered the car over on the side of the road and pointed to an old farm house that was sitting high up on a small hill surrounded by pecan trees and one lone magnificent magnolia tree. "I have seen pictures of that house over time. Some photographer has made it his life's work to record the

18

deterioration of that home place by taking pictures of it. Look at it now. I come here to visit it from time to time. It feels like an old friend. Do you know what I mean?"

I didn't have a clue, but I looked dutifully out the window and nodded the way Southern women often nod agreeably in response to questions about famous paintings in museums that are supposed to be admirable because they are famous (but really Van Gogh's dark painting of "The Sower" is just plain ugly!), about annual football games between longtime competitors and about which I don't care (if that's the thrill of victory or the heartbreak of defeat, I don't get that either), and in the produce department when someone asks me, "Is this cantaloupe ripe?" nodding happens then, too.

"That house reminds me of Faulkner's "A Rose for Emily". Do you remember the story?" Lovejoy moved his right arm out and slipped it loosely across the back of the front seat. His fingers toyed with the under curls at the back of my neck. I have a good bit of natural curl (been ironing and trying to straighten out my hair for years), and when I perspire those tendrils on the back of my neck don't just stand up, they spiral out of control. I was sweating and curling riotously about my forehead and at the back of my neck and hoping Lovejoy wouldn't feel the beads of perspiration there. So unladylike!

I concentrated on the magnificence of that magnolia tree. It was like I had never seen a magnolia tree before, but I had. This tree was different, alive, fulsome, pulsing with a kind of romantic aura that until that moment I had not experienced. The branches were full of the most marvelous white flowers. I marveled that whoever owned this tree must not have any socializing friends who needed flowers for tabletop centerpieces or it would have been more pruned of its sumptuous white blossoms and large waxy green leaves. Though the car window was tightly closed, I thought I could smell the blossoms from inside where the interior of the car was growing warmer. Mr. Lovejoy had turned off the engine and with it the air conditioner. I was hot.

"Make no mistake about what is on here," Lovejoy said softly, his voice a whispered confession in my left ear.

"The tree has so many flowers," I remarked, and my throat was now sandpaper dry. I couldn't remember the Faulkner story exactly, but I resolved to read it again soon so I could catch up with Mr. Lovejoy's observation.

His hand clasped the back of my neck lightly and one finger stroked the nape. My head ducked when he touched me. His other hand moved around my face. Using two cool fingers he tapped my chin and turned my face toward his.

"It isn't a complicated idea once you hear it. You didn't exactly hear me before, though I think you truly liked the bread pudding. I simply want you." And then he leaned forward and kissed me almost on the lips.

Startled, I moved my head slightly, and his kiss landed near the corner of my mouth instead. This has happened to me many times in my life, but I suspect, not often to Mr. Lovejoy. He did not lose his focus.

"What are you afraid of?" he asked, while he cocked his head and contemplated making another try at the kiss.

Lovejoy

I couldn't keep my head still any more than I could my right hand, which had begun to squeeze my thigh hard. I was trying to hold onto something: myself.

I stole a glance at him, considered the question to be a dare, and decided to call him on it. He eyed me quizzically, waiting for me to signal something else, so I smiled.

He kissed me again, and this time, I did not jerk away.

He smiled more to himself than at me after the second kiss, and if he had been a younger man, I would have considered that smile a show of conceit, but in the 12-year-old Buick beside an overladen magnolia tree next to a decrepit house that reminded him of Faulkner's story, I thought he just looked pleased with us both. I fought the urge to press my fingertips against my lips to see if the imprint of his mouth was still there, and after a while I could fight it no longer. That man could kiss, and as he drove us home, the memory of it ached. I turned my head to stare out the window so that he could not see my face and the mark of his lips on my mouth, which was burning.

Humming a Frank Sinatra song now, Lovejoy drove me back to my car where I had left it at the church and asked me if I would be present that night for evening Vespers. In a fit of self-preservation, I shook my head no, no, I would not be anywhere in his proximity, for by then the scent of him and the odd mix of safety and danger had caused me to fear for my life.

He smiled genially, a study in patience and optimism. I liked his mouth, the shape of his lips, the taste of mint and vanilla. My face was stony with these realizations of desire.

Back in my own car and as I drove away toward my home, I saw Mr. Lovejoy in the rear-view mirror, and he didn't wave or anything. He just remained there watching, standing guard by the church, and I thought of Fitzgerald's Gatsby, not Faulkner's Emily at all. I pressed the gas pedal hard, zooming away from his declaration of desire.

3

BE CAREFUL, IT'S MY HEART

I stayed home with the doors locked and the blinds closed. Lovejoy did not call me the next day. I ran my Monday errands and checked the phone for messages. Only Donald Trump had called asking for money, which is so strange because he tells the world he is rich.

No bouquet of flowers arrived from Mr. Lovejoy with a restatement of his intentions.

No love letter came in the mail on Tuesday containing a poem or words that celebrated my beauty or virtues. I decided that Mr. Lovejoy was a world-class flirt. I figured by Wednesday evening Elder Franklin Lovejoy would have forgotten what he had said to me and would be courting that woman whose laugh sounded like Christmas bells. He was probably talking to her now and buying her mimosas. Yes, it would be safe to go to the midweek service.

Telling myself that, I went to the Wednesday night fellowship supper and parked my car in my regular spot. When I entered through the side door, Frank Lovejoy was standing in the hallway, as if he had never left the church at all but had simply moved from the curb by the street to inside where he had been waiting for me since Sunday.

That's exactly what he said.

"I've been waiting for you, Gigi," he said.

"Hello, Love…." I said in a whisper I use in libraries and at funerals.

He was not wearing a tie. Men didn't wear ties on Wednesday nights. Instead, he wore a soft mint green cotton shirt with a narrow collar and some kind of khaki pants for which I don't have a name because I am ignorant of men's fashions. I don't have a brother, and I have never had a husband. My father has been gone five years now, but until his death he had worn heavy-duty work clothes purchased from a feed and seed store where farmers buy overalls. Dad had been the building superintendent of a local department store and had to wear clothes that could survive dirt, sweat, grit, fire, and climbing the building's flagpole when reaching the top was required.

I was sorrowfully noting my own ignorance about men's fashions as Lovejoy moved closer to me, automatically. The scent of him was soap and water and vanilla. The heat of his body was magnetic, like a fire in the hearth on a chilly day. The easy rapport bloomed within us again. I fell into walking right beside him. He placed his arm around my waist—I've always liked it when a man did that—and, he said, his voice a dusky rich timbre that promised intimacy and offered trustworthiness and other gallantries, "We're going this way, Gigi."

Lovejoy

It was the first night he used that nickname with me, and I didn't ask him why. It sounded French, and it was prettier than my name Cindy. Cynthia Louise Bell. Some people call me CeeCee, and the truth was I thought he had misunderstood that nickname. I liked Gigi better. It sounded like a girl who would drink mimosas on Sunday afternoon and do kissing in front of an ancient magnolia tree.

We walked down the long hallway together and toward the fellowship supper where we fell into line at the buffet with our friends. We made our plates while people around us—friends, all-- cut their eyes and nodded knowingly: two loose unattached people had found each other. If you have ever experienced that in the world, you know that all of society breathes a sigh of relief when two single people stop being a dangerous temptation to married people by joining up with one another.

I had experienced being seen as a danger to others off and on depending on my weight and hormones; but Lovejoy was a widower, and perhaps that experience of singleness as a cautionary tale was for him only two years old. His former wife had died year before last over the Christmas holidays, and I couldn't remember what she looked like or what had happened to her. I had an old church directory at home, and when I got back in my house, I would look her up and see for myself. I did remember that I had donated ten dollars in her memory to the memorial fund, which I do regularly for anyone who dies in my church because I am not good at writing condolence cards, don't usually know people well enough to visit their homes to express grief in person, and sending flowers for a funeral can run around eighty-five dollars. That's forty-three undrunk glasses of restaurant iced tea.

Mr. Lovejoy and I sat together during fellowship supper. We sang the three hymns together. He harmonized easily with "Jesus Loves Me, This I know" which is when I recalled that he had been in the choir way back when. I have at times wanted to join the choir but have always been afraid that I wouldn't know how to quit if I wanted to after I had started. Problems like that have caused me to sit in silence on the fringe of society in many different arenas for all of my adult life. The fact that Lovejoy had once sung in the choir and now didn't caused me to look at him with a deepening respect. He knew how to start, and he knew how to stop. Beside me, he sang harmony effortlessly.

When the preacher rose to give a homily, Mr. Lovejoy reached over and took my hand. I did not draw away. Instead, I listened halfway to Brother Dave's message and wondered if Mr. Lovejoy would kiss me again before the night was over. I wanted him to, and that is when I began to wake up to desire in a way I had never known it before. Until that moment desire had been more of a rumor. The reality of desire is very different than its reputation.

He saw me studying his mouth when I thought he wasn't looking, and he grinned and squeezed my hand; and whatever the preacher was saying, Mr. Lovejoy agreed out loud, fearlessly, unselfconsciously, "Amen." Only it didn't feel like to me in that moment that Frank was agreeing with the preacher. It felt like he knew what I was thinking, and he was agreeing out loud--making a promise of sorts to me. I was nervous and

Lovejoy

excited, feeling safe—dangerously safe. It was an expression I would use for our entire three-month courtship.

Mr. Lovejoy did not fail me. He kissed me later in the dark by my car and asked if he could follow me home to make sure I got inside safely. I couldn't tell him no. I didn't want to tell him no. All thoughts about his being an emissary of the church leadership to rebuke me for voicing unpopular opinions about not providing money and other forms of physical help to missionaries and poor people who needed expressions of tender mercy were laid to rest like Miss Emily's Homer. Yes, I had skim-read Faulkner's story but not read it closely. It was something about a prominent woman of the community marrying a man who was beneath her socially and most likely poisoned him with arsenic and then after he died kept him inside the house instead of burying him properly. It creeped me out. And I don't like Faulkner's long-winded sentences either. I felt it a shame that he hadn't been blessed with a better English teacher. God moves in mysterious ways.

Later that night after we had spent the evening talking about our lives and what we believe and what kind of music we liked, Lovejoy took me in his arms and kissed me with intention, exploring me in ways that no one had been curious about in a long time or maybe ever before. It felt new. It felt old. I was alive.

When he said, "Good night" he added with a gentle emphasis, "You are being courted."

I blinked in the dark, wondering how he knew just what to say to make me feel dangerously safe.

After Lovejoy finished saying good-night in all of the ways that an elder knows how to say them, I leaned against the door after I had locked it and knew that I would not be able to sleep. I stalled about going to bed, finding odd jobs to do to keep me moving around with my thoughts. I unstacked the dishwasher. I checked the voice mail twice though no one had called, but while I was by the phone I found the stack of old church directories.

Checking the dates of the years on the spines, I went back three years and opened the directory to the picture of Mr. and Mrs. Frank Lovejoy. And there she was: Amanda Lovejoy. She was pretty with a sweet plump sort of powdery face, soft brown hair, soft brown eyes, and she was not looking at the camera. Her head was slightly turned, and she was looking up at Frank the way all the women who tried to sit beside him at church looked up at Frank Lovejoy. Amanda looked at Frank the way that I looked at Frank now when I thought he couldn't see me soaking up his features. My gaze went from her to him and back again. They were a nice-looking couple. And she had died. He didn't. And now he was sitting next to me. The story of Lovejoy and me began to build itself like that in my mind though I had no one to tell the story to. Every now and then I wanted to open the old church directory and tell Amanda the story of Frank and me. I think Amanda alone would understand.

By our fifth dinner together we were almost inseparable. He didn't want to leave me. I didn't want him to go. When he went home after spending an evening with me, he called to say he was there safely, and he said other things in my ear in

28

a tone of voice so intimate, so irresistible that I had to keep myself in check. He wanted to know everything I thought— everything I'd ever done, how I lived, the schedule of my days and nights, why I was so often a volunteer and why I didn't have to earn a living. Parents and aunts and uncles have left me money. I did not add: "I am well fixed." Well-fixed means different things to different people. I didn't have to work. Interest from CDs and dividends from stocks were direct deposited into my checking account. I clipped a few coupons now and again, and I lived very simply so the money would last.

By the time of the next Tender Mercies meeting, I had almost forgotten that I was in the dog house with the Chairman, JD McGuffin. I walked right over to JD and hugged him when I entered the room. JD was shocked. Standing there he took that hug like a man. I laughed softly at him and myself, which is not a bad way to live and laugh about anything anywhere you go, even church.

I guess it would be shocking to be hugged by someone with whom you are irritated. I couldn't stop smiling at JD—at everyone. For the whole meeting, people who had been treating me carefully were smiling back, and twice, the men on both sides of me punched me in the arm when I voted *yes* and *yes*. If you have never been punched lightly on the arm by a man who is pleased with your presence, you have not experienced the bliss of belonging where you didn't belong before. I got punched in both arms and felt doubly blessed. I couldn't vote *no* on anything that night. I was happy. Everyone else seemed happy, too.

I went to my car alone under a starlit sky. Mr. Lovejoy was coming over at nine o'clock so that we could watch an old movie together. "Dodsworth" was one of his favorites. I was in a hurry but also patient. I wanted to be home, but I wanted to take my time getting there. I popped an old Frank Sinatra CD in my car's gizmo and sang along to "I've Got You Under My Skin," from Frank's album for Swingin' Lovers.

That same night Franklin Lovejoy asked me how I felt about marriage. I told him it wasn't for me.

He asked me to marry him. I said yes.

He wasn't surprised. Suddenly he was all business, extracting a small pocket calendar to look at dates. "Which days are good for you?"

"For what?" I asked. I had a busy week as usual. Housecleaning. Laundry. Car washing. Errand running. And I wanted to buy some art supplies. I wanted to draw everything I saw.

"I will make us an appointment to meet with the preacher. Pre-marital counseling."

I told him we were both too old to need counseling about our personal lives, and Frank said that he was too much in love with me not to seek it. If I wanted to be on the safe side, I would not turn down the opportunity to check what we both felt and wanted with a preacher. "Brother Dave is not in love with either of us," Frank said, grinning.

I said, yes, a synonym for amen. That was the only word I seemed to know how to say to Franklin Lovejoy.

4

I ONLY HAVE EYES
FOR YOU

Lovejoy told me that the preacher was probably postponing our meeting on purpose: "Giving us a cooling off period."

"Do we need to cool off?" I asked.

He grinned. "Maybe," he said.

He was flirting with me.

I turned my head away so that he couldn't see me smile.

"Meet you on our pew after Sunday school," he promised, taking a slow leave when he turned the corner toward his Sunday morning classroom.

Lovejoy wasn't teaching. The men in the class took turns teaching, and that morning, JD, the chairman of the Tender Mercies committee, was supposed to lead a discussion about that book that once you read it you have to become a missionary. It's that powerful! Two different people had given me that same book, and I always gave them my "Yes, your cantaloupe is ripe," Southern woman smile.

That book is famous for twisting arms and changing lives. Once you read it, you can't not become a missionary. I've read it twice, but I'm still right here—not a missionary.

Once upon a time before I knew Lovejoy, I had been in on a missionary interview where the man who was seeking funding name-dropped the book as his justification to explain his call to the field. "I read that Piper book. I have to go on the mission field now," he said, pointblank.

Everyone nodded yes, but me. I said, because I couldn't not say it, "Just because he knows the secret handshake—has proven that he has read the Piper book by referring to it in a casual way and perhaps with a wave of his hand that signals inevitability-- doesn't mean he's an authentic member of the non-tentmaker called-by-God-to-the mission-field club. It just means he's read the book, knows its reputation, and is using that slogan about the persuasive powers of the book to convince others to pay his living expenses."

The mission chair explained, "The oversight committee in Atlanta has approved his application, and he also took the personality profile test. Passed with flying colors."

"Don't the powers-that-be in Hot-Lanta get a percentage of what the missionaries raise as their support?"

"Yes."

I shrugged, and added, "Well, there seems to be something in it for everyone, and as far as that personality profile test goes, it's not so hard to fake being normal in the South. We have a lot of practice here." I looked around the room and initiated my nod-of-good-will, but no nods of agreement came in response to mine. It was a familiar feeling.

My words hit the others hard. Glances were exchanged. Sighs exhaled. I waited for someone to argue with me that night, but no one did. They didn't argue with me because they agreed with me. It was because they thought I was so hardhearted and hard headed that no one could reason with me. Realizing I had gone too far that night, I inched out of my chair in a kind of half crouch, ultimately pushing my own chair back up against the table and then slipping out the door no one else uses so I could get to the parking lot and my car without having to make more conversation.

Once I was inside my car, I told God, "I really need to shut up. I don't know why I won't."

As usual, God didn't answer me. People told me that God talked to them all the time, but he doesn't talk to me. I don't blame him, really. No one likes a Southern woman who is hard to get along with. My only saving grace is that I was just at that age when others naturally blamed contrariness on menopause.

No one would say that to my face, but they would speak about it in a kind of shorthand behind my back. While they might be a little right about the change happening to me, they would have been wrong about my saying what I said as if it were a new and cynical idea fueled by angry hormones.

Menopause isn't responsible. I have always thought this way. I just haven't let myself say the words out loud before. It was Mr. Lovejoy saying those "amens" on Sunday morning that had tapped into my inner Paul Revere; and when I speak up, I find myself calling out-- telling others the truth.

They just didn't like what I said. And I couldn't seem to make myself stop.

I was just about to fix a pleasant smile on my face to tamp down the unpleasant memory and associations regarding that Piper book episode, when I saw Judy and Susan walking my way in order to say a tight "Hello," which is the kind of greeting the other girls and I have been exchanging. That didn't happen. Instead, they both hurried over to me and steered me with eyes darting this way and that into the ladies' lounge.

A resting area affixed to the restroom, the lounge usually draws tired older ladies who need a time out between Sunday school and church and also nursing mothers who have recklessly tried to nurse their newborns in the Sunday school class with their bosoms exposed. It didn't matter that a nursing mother had draped a thick blanket over her chest and the nursing baby. Others objected to the idea of a single naked bosom being possibly on display in a Sunday school class (or even the idea that a towel could move and suddenly, uh-oh, there it is, a naked bosom, we've never seen one of those before even though it was a class full of women only!). So after a lot of squeaky chairs being pulled away from a nursing mother in a Sunday school class and resolute posture and frozen faces studiously not looking at her, young mothers with hungry infants learned to take themselves to the lounge where, strangely, the same women who were so uncomfortable in a classroom with her while nursing, would sit right beside her in the lounge and make amiable small talk about motherhood, babies, and the men we love who drive us crazy. That last part is an ongoing theme in the ladies' lounge, though if you listen closely, the revelations about men who drive you crazy are more boast than complaint and the intensity of the feelings is more about pride in being desired than a desire for it to ever stop.

Judy immediately went over to the three stalls. Leaning over she checked for feet. Just as I was thinking how agile she was—bending over like that, her expensively styled hair tumbling down close to her ankles, she stood upright, nodded to Susan and to me, and announced, "All clear."

Susan motioned toward the ancient sofa. Curious and immediately on guard, I sat down on the sofa where the young mothers who are breastfeeding usually sit. Judy went to the door and looked out again, said something to a friend, and then nodded meaningfully to Susan. I waited. The wives of two powerful elders, Susan and Judy didn't have much to say to me usually. There were real reasons for this.

In social terms they were my superiors. In female terms because of their married status and motherhood, they were my superiors. In terms of how many people liked them more than they liked me, it wasn't even close. Their funerals would be standing room only. Mine would be hosted in that small room where the very old who have out-lived all of their friends and most of their kinfolks are talked about by a preacher who has had to ask others for stories about who she or he was because he never met him or her. That's the room where they will have my funeral, and I can't imagine what anyone will say, probably something like, "She was here a long time, but she never really fit in. Bless her heart."

Though I prided myself on keeping my classic signature haircut which had made Farrah Fawcett famous and that I've worn since I was seventeen and classic clothes mostly from Talbots which used to be the outfit du jour for bank tellers, beside these two former cheerleaders my hair and clothes felt wrong. They were both thin and modern. I felt fat and out of date.

"We hear you are seeing Lovejoy," Susan announced abruptly. She sat upright comfortably, her posture easy while she habitually smoothed her pink poplin skirt, the hem of which landed just where it should in the middle of her knee. "We hear you are seriously seeing Lovejoy."

The small sofa upon which I was sitting heaved, sagging with my weight toward the floor. I instantly thought of a story that could be truthfully told at my funeral. For most of my life outdoor swings have broken beneath me, chairs have snapped underneath me, and sofas like the one I was on which had been holding up other women for years, sagged deeper and deeper to the floor. I am not drastically heavier than other people, but things break underneath me. Someone could tell that story at my funeral and let others draw their own conclusions.

I moved the position of my feet to change my balance. Susan was fine. Actually, she didn't seem to notice. But Judy did, moving to stand closer to both of us with her back to the door. I saw our reflections in the mirror over the sink. Judy was shorter in the mirror than she looked in real life.

"This old thing is too old for all of us," Judy said, stretching out her right hand to the back of the sofa. "The next time someone dies and leaves their estate to the church, we need to look for a replacement couch for this one. I will personally shove this one to the street."

"I'll help you," Susan offered immediately. They were that kind of friends-- instantly on each other's side.

But the words meant something else too. Her words were just buying time. Women talk like that, darting from one idea to another; but all the while, they have a destination toward which they are moving.

Susan's left hand moved forward and patted me on my left leg. "You're one of us, Cindy. And we couldn't know what we know without telling you before it's too late."

"What we sort of know," Judy said, interrupting. "But we don't have facts, exactly."

Susan pressed on, not needing to add the caveats that Judy felt compelled to offer. She said firmly, giving Judy a knowing glance that caused her to press her lips in an uncharacteristic grimace. "We know about Lovejoy, and we weren't sure anyone else had tried to tell you about him."

"Tell me what?" I asked. What could you know that I don't know? And so, I almost said, 'He's a very good kisser. And his hands. His grip. He is solid and strong. His voice can make you melt inside, and his smile is easy—it dawns on you. That's his smile. And Lovejoy likes to drink mimosas on Sunday. His eyes laugh when he's most serious, and he has a pleasant humming voice. All the songs he hums are love songs.' I would have told them everything in a great gush of exultation, the way girls do when they are in love, but something in the seriousness of their faces clued me in that this wasn't girl talk.

This was something else—something important enough that a temporary truce on a churchwide informal shunning of me had been called in order to deliver this caveat.

Susan maintained a steady gaze on me and said, as if she were delivering a weather report: "Lovejoy has a way with the ladies, and it's not always good for the lady."

Judy nodded vigorously. "Yes, CeeCee. Lovejoy has a way with women."

Not too many people called me CeeCee anymore, though sometimes people misremembered it and called me Cissy. Most people used my given name, Cynthia Louise Bell or Cindy Louise.

"We thought you might have heard; but in case you hadn't heard, we wanted—Susan and I felt that someone should tell you...."

"Warn you," Susan interjected.

"That Gigi told us right before she died that Lovejoy isn't what everybody thinks he is." She lowered her voice and repeated for emphasis: "Just before she died. Gigi died of a heart attack. Not a flicker of a warning either. Amanda was just here, and then she wasn't here anymore."

Her face grew stern with that pronouncement as if she blamed Amanda Lovejoy for her own death.

"Old Frank gets around, too, in case you didn't know," Judy said. "He was seeing Marjeen until he started dating you, and he stopped, suddenly, just like that," she said, snapping her fingers. They were well manicured, and polished with a mauve shade that looked good with most outfits. When I go to shop for that color of nail polish at the drugstore, I can never find it.

"It could happen to you. We just wanted you to know what Amanda said. And what Marjeen experienced. Gigi said Lovejoy is not what everyone thinks he is."

"Gigi?" I asked, my mouth going suddenly dry. My hands grew cold and still in my lap, and the waistband on my pants rolled down a smidge. I needed adjusting, and I couldn't do it with them in the room too.

"Yes. Gigi was Frank's pet name for his wife. What do they say about nicknames? There's a theory about nicknames and what the speaker intends by using them," Judy asked turning to Susan. "Is a nickname a term of endearment or a term of diminishment? I can't remember."

Susan shrugged. "Oh, people have all kinds of theories. Don't worry about that, sugar." She flashed Judy a quick apologetic grin for calling her "sugar" and added: "Amanda said Gigi was his special name for her." Leaning closer, Susan added, her eyes squinting in perplexity, "She said it was his special name for her given to him by God."

"His name for her given to him by God," I repeated dumbly. The couch was sagging closer to the floor, dropping deeper and deeper beneath me. My heart was going with it.

"When all is said and done, Lovejoy could be just fine," Judy said. "The men all like him. I've never heard my husband say a word against him. Usually if something is wrong with a man other men know it and will tell you, but our husbands haven't said anything against him."

"And it may be that Frank is just an ordinary man, no more, no less."

"The men have been using that word as a defense lately for all kinds of plans that have gone awry. ("What do you expect? I'm just an ordinary man!") You can sweep a lot of sin under that rug called ordinary," Susan interjected. And then, surprised to hear herself telling the truth in front of me and not just her best friend Judy, she regrouped. "And we are sorry for being a kind of messenger about this and all. But we wanted you to know that someone who was in a position to know him well said Old Frank isn't what he seems," Susan interjected, which is what Christians do when they have slandered someone and want to build in an escape explanation if they are wrong.

"And then she died of a heart attack," Judy repeated.

"That doesn't have anything to do with what we are saying," Susan said.

"But now another woman in the church-- Marjeen has her own story to tell, but she's not saying much. Her feelings are kind of hurt right now, and she, well, of course, she doesn't like you, which is understandable, I mean, given the circumstances. Lovejoy was with her. Then he wasn't. Her disliking you actually isn't personal, if you know what I mean," Judy said.

"No. She doesn't like you. Not a bit," Susan affirmed.

"I don't even know Marjeen. I mean, I've seen her around, but I don't know Marjeen."

"Well, anyway, Katie is holding the door for us so we can have this little chat with you. We've all got to get to Sunday school in five minutes, but Judy and I, well, we are the president and the vice president of the women's auxiliary, and we felt it was our duty…,"

"Our sisters-in-Christ duty," Judy agreed instantly. "Because when all is said and done, you are one of us just like Marjeen."

"And Gigi," Susan said solemnly. "God rest her soul."

"To tell you what we had heard."

"But of course, you know yourself and you know best for yourself."

And before I could agree or disagree with that idea, the two women in the church stood up, walked to the two adjacent sinks, washed their hands again as if they were washing their hands of the subject now. With a quick glance at me still sitting on the sagging floral couch, Susan tugged slightly on the door. Katie let go of the knob on the other side, and then the three of them went off to the Sunday school class together while I remained in the lounge on the sofa which had died beneath me.

The door closed softly after them with a thud, and I hummed that Perry Como song as they walked away. No one else came in, but then Sunday school classes were beginning all over the church. Everyone with a place to be was in one of them.

I couldn't move. I sat there thinking about whether I needed to leave town, but move where? My chest hurt. Was I going to die? What kind of funeral would they give me? Would Marjeen come? Lovejoy? Susan and Judy? Was a nickname a term of endearment, diminishment, or just a name you used so that you didn't have to remember someone's real name because there had been so many ladies....so many ladies. *And it's not always good for the ladies.*

I don't know how long I sat there, but after a while I heard the choir upstairs begin to practice the Call to Worship number. Then they sang a song that must have been planned for the Offertory. Voices began to sound in the hallway, and that's when I realized that I had never gone to Sunday school and that Lovejoy had. Now he would be making his way to our regular pew for the eleven o'clock service and would be waiting for me.

My purse was on the floor. I took it over to the mirror where I could go through my primping routine. I daubed on some rose satin lipstick—smoothed my hair with the fold-up brush I keep in my purse. I leaned in and looked closer. I had liked the blond streaks this morning, but now they caught the light in the lounge and looked a little brassy. *Cheap. Trying to look younger than I am. These days I look better in shadows and candlelight,* I thought sadly. I tugged on my pants and pulled them up to my waist, touching the button to make sure it was holding. My clothes felt too tight, and my chest hurt. I pressed my right hand on the middle between my breasts and felt my heart racing. *Was I having a heart attack? Love hurts. Being in a church hurt. Not having women friends who are really your friends hurts. I missed my mother.* I didn't know what to do and was thinking about just walking out the side door and going home—someone would see me and give me a ride, I know a lot of people! —but before that idea worked itself out, the bathroom door opened and in came Marjeen.

42

Lovejoy

She stared hard at me for a full five seconds, and then went to the sink where she busied herself primping and washing her hands. We traded nods and inconsequential murmurs. It was in the murmuring—*nice day, yes, nice day*, that I knew what the warning from Susan and Judy was all about: Marjeen had been jilted, and she was jealous. I remembered something else too. Susan and Judy were Marjeen's friends, not mine. It was simple to understand, really. Her friends were trying to run me off so that Marjeen could have Lovejoy back. Women takes sides, and the women I knew always took another woman's side over mine.

I smiled sweetly, then—my mind made up. I wasn't giving up or slinking out the side door. That's just what they were hoping for.

"Bye-bye!" I told Marjeen gaily, and left the dying couch and the echoes of the conversation.

Back in the corridor that led to the sanctuary, I wended through the milling congregants, holding my head up high and my purse in front of me for protection. I felt that I needed protection. I believed that everyone around me thought Marjeen was the better choice for Lovejoy and young enough that he could call her his trophy wife. But I didn't believe it. When I saw Lovejoy waiting for me by our pew in the sanctuary, I walked right over and kissed him on the mouth in front of God and everyone else.

Lovejoy blotted his mouth as he ushered me into the pew beside him, and he breathed in my ear, "You're adorable."

If we had been home on the couch watching an old movie, he would have bitten my ear lobe. He didn't in church, but he could have, and I wouldn't have minded.

I sat down firmly beside him and read the scripture assigned for the day's sermon. It was from the Song of Solomon about the nature of desire and longing, and it couldn't have been more appropriate.

5

STRANGER IN PARADISE

Like all married people who think all single people should get married, Dave the preacher could not have been more pleased that Lovejoy and I had found each other-- even though he began the conversation with a twinkle in his Calvinistic eye to soften his admonishment, "No more kissin' in the pews, Cindy."

I didn't know what he was talking about at first, and then I did. Lovejoy reached over, patted my hand, and said, "She's adorable."

My face burned. I had kissed Lovejoy in public in church. It was also the first time I had initiated a kiss. I should have remembered that sooner. The memory sobered me. *What was I becoming?* I wondered if I was losing my mind.

And then the conversation began—the one called pre-marital counseling. There were many questions, and it felt like a test. I have never been good at taking tests, so I put on a budding magnolia smile—sweet as can be. *I'm paying attention. I'm not afraid. I believe that everything will be just fine. Honey, your cantaloupe is ripe and so are your tomatoes.*

That's the expression I used. Lovejoy continued to hold my hand.

"Remind me, how many times have you been…. bereaved, Frank," the preacher asked.

"Twice bereaved," Lovejoy replied succinctly.

I knew about one wife, the other Gigi. The news of another dead wife caused me to smile differently, glassily in self-defense. I squeezed Frank's hand to console him over his double loss while inside of me my thoughts froze. I was aware that I needed to think, but I couldn't. I swallowed hard and wondered what I was supposed to say when I could speak.

"Rectal cancer took the first wife, Darla," Lovejoy said. "Cardiac arrest stole my second. Sweet Amanda. Back in the day, doctors didn't know much to do about rectal cancer," he announced. His voice was too loud for the room. "And Amanda had a heart attack at 3 pm in my prayer closet where she was ironing my clothes. That girl loved to iron."

He said the words *rectal cancer* easily, and I was embarrassed by the words. I hoped he wouldn't bring up his first wife Darla very often.

"Praying didn't save Darla or Amanda, so it was God's will is what it was, and that is that." His hands moved automatically. He released my hand and let his fall on either side of him. "The Lord giveth and the Lord taketh away. Blessed be the name of the Lord."

"And, remind me, how many times have you been married, Cindy?" the preacher asked.

I was startled by the question because Dave the preacher had known me twenty years. I thought he knew me, but he didn't—not really. I knew far more about him than he did about me. I knew that he was close to burning out from time to time. I know that his heart had been broken by people who were supposed to be a good neighbor. I know that he has looked in the mirror and seen the ruddy complexion of a healthy young man become the drawn pale look of a pastor who has helped to bury family members of people he loves more than is good for him to love. I wanted to tell him right then, "I know you love people and that you are a real preacher. I know that." But I didn't. It was his turn to talk; and as usual, it was my turn to listen.

I had been listening to Dave preach for years, but this was the first conversation we had had about a personal subject. My feelings were hurt that he didn't know the answer, and nervously I wanted to say but didn't: *Have you ever seen me sitting next to a man to whom I was married? Have you not even seen me sitting out there listening to you preach the Good News?* So far nothing said in this meeting felt like good news to me. Not even a little bit.

"Never married," I replied, and it felt like I failed a test right then.

To be unmarried in the South is a kind of failure. To be divorced is another kind of failure. But to have never been married, well, that is the worst kind of failure. No one must have ever wanted me. The only women in a worse position than people like me were jilted women. I had a friend whose husband inexplicably and dramatically left her. After that, she had terrible health problems, and people loosely associated his leaving her with the idea that something was wrong with her. Then, once she began to get so very sick, others treated her with great sympathy but also with a kind of suspicion: *Really. What is wrong with her?* The unspoken conclusion and commentary were: *No wonder he left. There must have been something wrong with her, and he saw it first and ran for his life. Bless his heart. Bless her heart*

An uncomfortable silence occurred. The preacher, younger than we though old enough to think and insistent on doing his duty by us, went on to his next question working from memory through his litany of pre-marital counseling questions that accrued the information that would result in my passing the test: 'Could I get married in the church to this God-fearing twice bereaved elder who probably deserved better than a woman no man has ever wanted before?'

I spied a piece of paper with numbered questions on it positioned on the corner of Dave's desk. Before I could read it upside down, the preacher asked, "Have you discussed the age difference?"

"I'm fifty, almost," I said.

"And I am older by a long shot," Lovejoy said with a self-deprecating grin. "And look at her trying to sound older just to catch up with me. She's younger," Lovejoy said firmly. "But I'm not exactly robbing the cradle."

"I hadn't noticed an age difference," I admitted honestly.

"In time you might. There are differences between generations," the preacher said, and he sat back in his chair waiting for Lovejoy or me to say something.

Lovejoy crossed his legs, and his salmon-colored silk socks peeped out of his tan pants legs. I was slightly uncomfortable by the sight of the pink socks, and I didn't know why. A number of Lovejoy's summer dress shirts were in different pastels: light pink, light blue, minty green, a dusky yellow. Lovejoy had all kinds of colorful bow ties and matching socks. He had two slightly different summer suits: one a seersucker and the other a kind of tan linen blend. All the shoes he wore had a waxy sheen—good leather well-polished. Since we had been keeping company I had been washing and ironing my clothes more than I ever had before, and checking the straps of my bras and slips. I had thrown away more old underwear than I knew I had been keeping. In a frenzied state last Saturday afternoon, I had replenished my intimates, shaking my head at the options available to women now. Some of the choices in the lingerie department had scared the fool out of me. The less cloth involved the more they cost. Animal prints on lingerie made me terribly nervous. What had happened to pink and cream and gold satin and lace?

I spoke up nervously. "The other day Frank was humming a song, and I knew it was an old Perry Como song. I think it was, 'Don't let the stars get in your eyes, don't let the moon break your heart....' That's what you were humming." I turned to Lovejoy for confirmation.

"Was I?" Lovejoy asked me, ruminatively. "I haven't thought of that song in years—don't know why I was humming it."

I did not add that I had been humming it ever since.

The preacher seemed unaffected by the mention of an old song. I wondered how many revelations between couples he had heard during pre-marital counseling and if that was the great benefit to the couples: questions asked and all kinds of answers leaking out, some helpful, others irrelevant.

"Taste in music is one kind of subject. But have you discussed your finances? Do you know how you will share bills? Where you will live?"

We had not discussed any of it—nothing at all. I didn't care. As long as I was sitting next to Lovejoy with his hand on my thigh, I did not care where I was or where I lived.

"Sometimes at your ages, a pre-nuptial agreement and updated wills are a good idea, especially if you have previous wills where you have made earlier decisions to leave your holdings to people you have loved before and built an earlier family with."

"I've got a will," I confessed readily. I am a big believer in not dying without a will, in having insurance, in owning a pre-paid funeral, and I actually have an extra grave plot bequeathed to me by my parents who believed until the days of their respective deaths that one day I would finally marry. I had just been waiting on the right man to want to spend eternity next to me. I was just about to mention the extra grave plot as if it were a version of a hope chest, when it occurred to me that Lovejoy might already be planning to be buried next to one of his previous two wives. I stifled the surprise still inside of me over the first wife, Darla. Then there was Amanda. Only he had called Amanda Gigi. What had he called Darla? Darling? And both wives had died. The thought hit me hard. Very hard. I began to hum softly the Perry Como song—*Don't let the stars get in your eyes don't let the moon break your heart*-- until I heard myself, and then I stopped.

"My will is up to date. Assorted charities. The church," Lovejoy replied airily. "Perhaps a fine-tuning of our respective wills and if you like a pre-nuptial agreement would be wise, considering...."

A pre-nuptial agreement. I thought those only existed on TV where people were very rich. *Was Lovejoy rich?* I looked at him anew, curious, and the strangest idea began to grow inside of me: 'I can drink iced tea at any restaurant any time I like any day of the week.' I grinned broadly. Unlimited sweet iced tea with lemon. Cloth napkins, too.

As this daydream took hold, the preacher said thoughtfully, "Harold would do a pre-nup for you both, gratis, if you like. It's his spiritual gift to the church—to manage pre-nuptial agreements, and he will even update a will for a love gift to missions. The pre-nup would be just a standard contract that you share your incomes-- what you have while married, but if one of you walks out, then you take with you out the door what you brought into the marriage. I don't like to talk about pre-nups more than you do or divorce, but divorce happens. It happens a lot," the preacher said tiredly. "Vows aren't what they used to be," Dave said, with a kind of beleaguered wonder in his voice.

And then I saw what others had whispered to me. His left eye drifted lazily toward the wall. Dave has a lazy eye. I had never seen his eye do that before. He must have been tired. We had tired him. I wanted to apologize for making his left eye do that. But I listened instead.

"That sounds reasonable," Lovejoy agreed readily.

"I don't care one way or the other," I answered honestly.

Lovejoy patted my hand, and I wanted to go home. For the first time since we had been dating, I wanted to go home alone. I promised myself to think about that later. And what Judy and Susan had said. And Lovejoy had had two wives, and he said the words "rectal cancer" very loudly and too easily. Really. And he had about a dozen bow ties that I knew about, and his socks were prettier than mine. My feet were getting cold.

Then the questions changed. They got personal. The preacher began to smile more, and when the secretary buzzed him and reminded him that he had a meeting in ten minutes, I knew that she had been asked to buzz him and his reminder of the next meeting was an exit from this one, which was mostly routine for Dave and probably Lovejoy, while the meeting had been sheer torture for me.

Still the preacher asked his questions, his hand holding a pen that had bite marks on the top. Did he chew on his pen? Was he a reformed smoker? Sometimes people who chewed pens were reformed smokers. Or maybe it was someone else's pen with bite marks and he was just holding it ready, in case he needed to write a note. But the preacher never wrote down anything about us. Dave finally got to his closing questions.

"What is Cynthia to you?" he asked Lovejoy.

"The woman I want," Frank replied without hesitation.

My identity enlarged.

"What is Frank to you?" the preacher asked me next.

I studied Lovejoy, saw his coat sleeve barely covering the cuff of his pale pink shirt, recalled the feel of his hand around my waist, his vanilla mint breath mixed with mine, his resolute strength, the intoxicating sensation of danger and safety, and I answered as truthfully as I knew how: "I have been waiting for Franklin Lovejoy my whole life."

"If this isn't a love match, I don't know what is," the preacher declared.

The preacher reached out and took our hands and placed them together—a practice move that he would make later at the conclusion of the formal wedding ceremony when he pronounced us husband and wife. Turning toward Lovejoy, he said, "Frank, congratulations." And when Dave turned to me, he said, "Cindy, you will make a beautiful bride. I guess you will be cutting back on your volunteer work. Married women don't have much time to be on committees. At least, not for a while anyway," he added, and then Dave laughed and said, "May I kiss the bride?"

And before I could say yes, and I would have, Dave the preacher leaned over and kissed me on the cheek. It was his way of apologizing for calling a halt to my kissing Lovejoy in the church pew in public, and I forgave him everything he had ever said from the pulpit that I had been unable to ever say amen to because I didn't agree with him. It is easy to turn the other cheek for a kiss.

The two men traded knowing smiles, and I retreated inwardly, moving toward the security of Lovejoy. The preacher approved of the move, and Lovejoy did not shift away.

We got married two weeks later in a low-key ceremony that took place in the same room where the small funerals are hosted. Then my husband took me to the Grand Hotel in Point Clear, where we watched the sun set together. Just as it disappeared beneath the horizon, Lovejoy kissed me deeply as he had hinted he would on the first date during that drive in the country.

6

BEWITCHED, BOTHERED
AND BEWILDERED

Six weeks into our honeymoon and after I had discovered the reality that bliss was possible and happiness something more than a good night's sleep, I decided I had made the best decision of my life.

My emotions were new and grew so quickly I could not categorize them. I learned love as the days progressed. Life with Lovejoy was intense. I almost didn't recognize myself—my feelings. Everything about me was measured in terms of him. My every thought tracked his movements from morning to night. The closer he was, the happier I was. When he moved away, the light left the room. Darkness came.

In our seventh week of married bliss, Frank awakened earlier than usual. I felt him stir, felt the weight of the bed shift, felt the heat of him move toward the doorway, and rumpled with ease and remembered desire and a satisfaction that was still new to me, I felt him leave our room. I felt cold. I closed my eyes and waited for the urgency of loss to touch him and cause him to return—I needed him! -- but Lovejoy didn't come back.

Waiting for him I drifted off to sleep, and when I woke up an hour later, he was gone from the house.

The coffee was old in the coffee pot and lukewarm. I looked about for a note and found one. "Be back by lunch. Wait for me."

Without thinking, I pressed the note to my lips, knowing that no woman my age did things like that. I felt silly and also pleased with myself, ate a piece of toast, and then dressed as if I were going to a fancy event. It was, sort of. It was lunch with my Lovejoy.

He arrived by 11:00 and waved away my questions about a meeting at church. Instead, he pointed to a picnic basket and said, "I'm taking you to the lake for lunch to celebrate. We have an offer on your house. If all goes well, the realtors and the lawyers will close in a month. You'll be completely moved in here. Whatever will happen next?"

It was a question he had taken to asking, his grey-blue eyes amused with the prospect of a future that was unfolding in front of us like a happy adventure. I had been going back and forth between his house and mine. As long as he was nearby, I didn't care where I lived or slept. He was a man in charge of "keeping us headed in the right direction," and so he wanted this loose end called my house to sell.

He was happy about it. It couldn't have mattered less to me. I smiled and watched him be in the room. He moved with ease and confidence. He was amused by my watching him. Every now and again I heard Susan or Judy whisper in my memory, "Lovejoy has a way with the ladies" and I always answered right back. "Yes, he does, and I like it."

Lovejoy

*****

It was more than a drive to the lake fifty miles away. It was more than a lunch. Frank had hired a boat. He cranked up the engine and steered us with a smile on his face that reminded me of the one he wore on our honeymoon while standing on the pier looking at the water. He steered us safely out of the marina and around a corner to a small inlet that he knew about. We traveled in silence for a while. It was very peaceful. The water was calm and blue and the sky big and clear. He moved the wheel gently with confidence, and I felt like I was dancing with him on the water. Hours or minutes later—I didn't know which--he anchored the boat, and there we had lunch with the slow movement of the water beneath us and the air smelling fresh. Afterwards, he seduced me under the blue sky on a thick blanket that was clean and folded and ready for us in the boat. While I was gazing up, a bird flew by and I remember thinking: 'I'm flying, too. I'm alive. I wasn't before.'

I moaned his name. His hands moved—his body hovered in the air above me. He nuzzled my neck. "Happy?" he asked, sitting up and looking about him.

So happy I almost couldn't breathe, I nodded. When I didn't answer him, he turned and looked at me. "You are happy, aren't you? I want you to be happy more than anything on this earth."

Sitting up, I leaned my head against his back and moved my hand around his chest and felt his heart beating. He was warm and sticky and breathing and alive. "I am happy," I promised him.

Rising, he gathered the picnic things and put them back in the basket. "When the house closes, what do you want to do with the money?"

"I don't care," I told him honestly. "I have everything I want."

"Do you want me just to take care of it?"

"I do," I said, mimicking my vows. I liked saying those words.

Our eyes met, and for an instant, I thought he might stretch out again beside me on the blanket and we could watch the birds fly by again, but he didn't.

"I better get you home," he said.

Back in the car, he drove silently, his mind working now, his focus more intense on the road while I nestled against him, my head on his right shoulder. Every now and then Frank rolled his shoulder slightly, but he didn't complain about the weight of me. Eventually, I shifted back to my side of the car.

"Do you mind if we stop by the church for a few minutes? I am expecting something in the mail."

"At the church?"

He nodded, I think. I wasn't looking. I said I would wait in the car while he went inside, but then I needed to go inside and freshen up. I didn't see him in the church office, but I could hear two men talking down the hallway. I stopped at the lounge and then went looking for him, deciding as I drew closer to the sound of his voice that he might not like for me to hunt him down in front of his friends, like a clinging wife, a stalker. The thought of embarrassing him embarrassed me. I stopped and turned, preparing to go back to the car and be found just as he left me when I heard him, his resonant voice carrying down the hallway right to me though he was speaking to a man. "Women love to be distracted with romance. That's always true. You can take it to the bank."

"I can take it to the bank," I repeated, hurrying back down the hallway toward the car. He found me looking just as he had left me, but I was different. *Women love to be distracted with romance.*

He reached out his hand and took mine, squeezed and asked, smiling, "What are you thinking?

"About the lake and the bird and the water," I replied.

"And me?" he inquired. His hand moved to my thigh. His fingers gripped me.

"You are all I think about," I told him honestly, and he looked satisfied, taking the turn toward his house, our house. "Did you get the mail you were expecting?"

"Mail?" he asked, before remembering. "I didn't mean mail. I meant a message, and yes, I had a quick chat too with a deacon who was having trouble at home. You know how they come to older men to talk about matters. I don't know if I was any help."

"I bet you were," I said quietly, shifting in the seat to look at him. He was a handsome man who looked as good in the shadows as he did in the bright sunlight.

Later that night, we made love again for the second time in a day. He patted my thigh again as he had in the car before rising in the night to take care of a matter he had forgotten: "We are still on our honeymoon. I hope it lasts forever," he said, as he left.

He didn't come back to bed. I fell asleep, waking up at daylight to find him sitting beside me holding a cup of coffee from which he had been drinking.

I roused, pulled myself upright, looked about for my cotton night shift, found it and wrestled it over my head. He handed me the half-empty cup of coffee. I watched him over the rim of the coffee cup. He looked content.

"I'm going out—will be gone most of the day. What are you going to do?"

"Housework," I said.

He nodded approvingly. "Get out of the house. Go for a walk. It's good for your joints."

"My joints are working fine," I said, struggling to rise.

He pressed me back. "I'll get you a fresh cup."

"I need to get up."

"In a minute," he said. He was gone less than that, bringing with him fresh coffee and wrapping my fingers around it while pressing his hand on top of mine. For a moment, I wondered if he would come back to bed. I scooted over. He didn't notice my invitation.

He had his public face on. "You do whatever you want to around the house. I'll be home around four o'clock. We'll go out to dinner. Have some wine. Do something with your hair."

"I always do my hair when we go out."

He had teased me about it the second week of our living together. "You wash your hair every day?"

"I wash my hands every day," I replied easily. I was flirting with him. It took me a moment to realize he wasn't flirting. And then I grew defensive. "I blow it dry and then either hot

60

roll it or iron it. I have some natural curl, and I don't sit under a hair dryer anymore."

I missed old fashioned beauty shop routines where you move from the hair wash station to the swivel chair and then to the hair dryer where you hear only the hum of the dryer and the sweet background noise of women telling their secrets to one another. It is very peaceful to sit under a hair dryer, tune out the world, and keep your secrets to yourself.

"And hairspray? You still use hairspray?"

"Doesn't everybody?" I replied.

"Not everybody," he said, amused. "But you could open the bathroom window when you spray your hair. That might help."

"Help what? I thought it smelled good."

He smiled politely and walked away. We hadn't talked about my hair since, but from then on when I used hair spray, I opened the bathroom window. That first time I opened the bathroom window while using hair spray, I finally focused on Amanda's swimming pool still covered in a blue tarp. Of course, I had noticed the pool before. I had heard Frank talking about what to do with the pool this year. He thought keeping the pool was unnecessary, an expensive luxury we didn't need to keep up. He wanted to fill in the pool and be done with the mess and the danger. "If some child wandered over here and drowned in our pool, we'd be liable."

"There aren't any children living around here," I said, though I didn't know that for sure. I hadn't seen any children. Frank didn't want the expense of the pool, but I felt differently. Having experienced fulfilled desire, I wanted more of what I wanted, and I wanted to go swimming. It was hot outside, and I didn't care about the cost. I wanted to dive into the cool waters of the pool and experience the water all around me and float on my back and feel the sun on my face and....

My daydream was cut short by Frank calling out, "I'll check in later."

I almost called out, "Don't go," but I didn't.

After I heard the door close, I rose and stripped the bed, peeling off my nightgown and underwear. Standing in front of the mirror, I looked at myself hard. We had been eating rich meals since the wedding, and three months before during our courtship we had eaten dessert at every meal. Life had been very sweet. I stepped on the scale. I had gained eight pounds. All the more reason to keep the pool and use it.

I remade the bed with fresh sheets, changed out the laundry, and puzzled over whether I would go for a walk or not. I didn't want to go. I preferred to sit in the living room and watch for Lovejoy to come home. Taking note of that longing in myself, I laughed softly, and said, strangely proud, "I'm in love, and I'm a fool."

To distract myself with something other than romance, I went to his office to dust, and that is where I saw his Day-Timer open to the day. He kept a portable version of it in the breast pocket of his suit. The one on his desk wasn't hidden. The notes to himself were written in a kind of shortened code.

I looked at the day's schedule: Church. Decide donations to distribute.

I flipped the pages backwards to our day at the lake. Take Gigi on outing. Eat lunch. Mk luv. Sl deal.

Lovejoy

I paged backwards, finding other days and occasions where romance had occurred with similar notes to himself: reminders of how I had been distracted by romance.

A cold sensation began in my chest and moved throughout my body. I paged all the way back to the first time he had taken me to the Country Club. "Make date. Slv problem. Marry?" I looked at that question mark. *What was that question doing there*?

I backed slowly away from his office, snagging my purse. With no destination in mind, I got into my own car for the first time since I had married Lovejoy. It cranked just fine, and it felt normal backing out of Amanda's driveway, though it was trickier than the one at my house that had just sold.

My house! Why weren't we living in my house? Strangely, I hadn't thought much about my house other than to pack boxes randomly to transport personal items to the two bedrooms that Lovejoy told me were available "to boarders who qualify."

I thought he was being cute. I laughed. I said, "Do I need references?"

And then he had pulled me to him and said looking right into my eyes, "I know exactly who you are."

His answer had sent a shiver down my spine—caused a shock of intensity as if he thought I was somebody more dangerous than I am—just an ordinary Southern woman who had grown up in the neighborhood. Look at me now.

"Look at me now," I said as I slowly drove over to my old house. The sign in the front yard read, "SOLD." What a success that word *sold* suggests. Change. Improvement.

Progress. The yard looked nice. The driveway had been power washed. The gutters had been cleaned out. Lovejoy had recruited the labor, drawing it from the deacons who kept a list ready to provide answers for questions like his. "Do you want me to just take care of it?"

He had asked that question repeatedly, often, and as if I were being hypnotized, I had said, *yes, yes, thank you, yes.* Sitting in the car next to my abandoned house--for that is how it felt-- I wondered how I had said yes so readily and so often. I was homesick all of a sudden and wondered if there was any way to change my mind and return to my house and my life where there were no distractions. At the very least I could walk through my parents' home for old time's sake. But when I considered the idea, my legs didn't want to get out of the car and a strange sensation occurred in my chest as if my heart were breaking. But a heart doesn't break over a house. It was just a house where I had grown older and alone. Yes, I had grown older and more and more alone. It had not been hard to move in with Lovejoy and leave the house behind. I hadn't really thought about my move until then. Not at all. I blinked back instant tears, marveling at how intense the distractions had been and my own unthinking response to Lovejoy's courtship of me and now our marriage.

What was I crying about? I wondered, as tears overflowed and ran down my face in a slow warm stream of confusion, despair, and a strange, strange grief over hearing the echo of my own *yes* repeating itself in my mind.

Unable to make myself go inside my old house and say a proper good-bye to my old life, I started the car and moved back out in the lane, going nowhere in particular, I thought, until I ended up at the small shopping center where a location of my bank occupied the corner near the traffic light. I almost never used this branch of my bank, but I parked and went inside and up to the nearest teller and introduced myself.

Then, extracting a checkbook and my driver's license to prove my identity, I said, "I want to check my balance and recent expenditures."

Stephanie was not interested in why I was asking initially. She seemed weighted down by her own problems. Behind her was the drive-thru window, and a black SUV eased up alongside the building.

"Scuse me," Stephanie said, spinning around on her rolling stool. Using her feet, she scooted over to the window and greeted the customer at the window.

"Just a deposit," the driver called out, before inserting the plastic tube with the deposit inside and sending it through the chute.

Stephanie concluded the transaction and then rolled herself back over to me.

"Why was the customer at the window more urgent than I am standing right here in front of you?" I asked.

"Can't let 'em get backed up out there. Causes traffic problems." That explanation suited Stephanie, so I stated my first request again, hoping another drive-thru customer wouldn't arrive to interrupt us.

"I want to see a list of recent transactions on this account," I said, showing Stephanie my checkbook.

She sighed as another car drove up and honked a rat-a-tat rhythm that once upon a time had these words to it: "A shave and a haircut two bits." Did other people know that the rhythm of those blasts used to have a meaning—used to be something more than a blast that demanded attention? They were only echoes now, sounds passed along from driver to driver—no one really knew except people who had lived long enough to say the words out loud.

Stephanie wanted to roll back over there immediately but didn't. Instead, she typed in my name and account number and turned her computer screen around so that I could see it.

"Y'all don't use e-payment from the bank yet," she observed, and there was judgment in her voice. "Do you want me to tell you how to do that?"

"Not right now," I replied, leaning toward the screen.

"You got utility payments and a couple of checks to the church."

"Can you make the picture of that check bigger?"

Stephanie leaned forward. Using her thumb and forefinger she touched the screen and made the image bigger.

I leaned forward and read the small line on the left. "Tender Mercies."

Stephanie looked over her shoulder nervously. "I got window people to take care of, and everybody," she said, letting impatience enter her voice. Or maybe she was scared she was going to get into trouble for not being able to wait on two people at once.

The check designated for Tender Mercies was for five thousand dollars. "Five thousand dollars," I said out loud. I no longer automatically computed amounts in terms of how many glasses of iced tea I could buy. I had been trying to teach myself to think differently. Even with that resolve, I still had to say the words. "That's two thousand five hundred glasses of iced tea. A lifetime of iced tea—gone just like that." I didn't snap my fingers. I didn't have that much energy and will in me.

"Is everything okay, Mrs. Lovejoy?" Stephanie asked, as the driver behind her drove on through.

Suddenly it was as if we were newborn allies, alive together in the common struggle to manage our different tensions and the calls of help from impatient customers and mysterious husbands.

I looked at Stephanie, whose gaze had warmed. She was suddenly present, alive in the moment with me. She reminded me of the man at the grocery store who carried my bags to the car, and how we always walked together, like we were old friends. But we weren't. How much of my life before Lovejoy was made up of alive-in-the moment encounters with other people just doing their jobs?

"I don't know," I said. "I don't know if I'm all right or not."

Stephanie nodded as if she understood that comment, and I felt no surprise in her when I, lost in my thoughts, abruptly turned and walked away. Suddenly chagrined by the realization of my own rudeness, I turned in the doorway to offer Stephanie a wave of farewell and gratitude, but she had already rolled back over to the drive-thru window and was speaking through the glass darkly to another stranger just about to pass through her life.

7

LOVE ME WITH ALL
OF YOUR HEART

Frank was waiting for me at home when I arrived.

"I'm early," he said unnecessarily. He waited for me to ask a question. When I didn't, he offered an assessment, "Things went well."

Distracted by what I had seen at the bank, I tried to pass Frank on my way to the shower. He was sitting in the recliner, and he tugged me down onto his lap. "How's my girl? How's my Gigi?"

"Why do you call me that?" I asked, wriggling. My legs were hanging awkwardly over the side of the recliner, and I felt eight pounds too heavy on his lap.

"I have my reasons," he said, his eyes twinkling. His breath smelled of lemon now and mint. He had been drinking iced tea, and he pressed his mouth to the side of my neck while his hands contained me.

"You feel all fresh and good," he whispered. "But I'm still taking you out to an early supper—the kind old people eat. That's what happened to you when you married me. You ended up going out to old people meals. They are called Early Bird specials."

"Nothing about you is old," I replied, pushing up.

He released me.

"Let's go out and order a steak, have some wine, eat a hot roll. Who knows what we'll do after that? We might even hold hands."

For the first time in weeks, I wasn't hungry—not a bit. I lied, "That sounds good. I didn't have lunch."

"Then you're hungry," he said, standing. He was looking at me, but his attention was elsewhere.

He stood guard in our bedroom while I showered. The door was slightly cracked, and he talked to me while I rinsed off. I didn't like that about married life, and no one in the ladies' lounge had ever complained about it. Other husbands didn't talk to their wives in the bathroom? He talked to me while I put on my face. "I'm having the pool cleaned and refilled just for you. It'll help you get out of the house some."

"That's good," I replied tersely as I commenced my make-up ritual: Merle Norman base make-up, blusher, eye shadow, eye liner, eye brows filled in, and then my lips were outlined in pencil before I smudged the lip color on my lips. Stepping back, I surveyed the effect. I looked like myself, but I didn't feel like myself.

Lovejoy walked over and kissed me on the back of my neck and whispered in my ear, "Life is short. Meet you by the front door in fifteen minutes."

"Twenty," I said. At least twenty. I still hadn't done my hair

Lovejoy

I opened the bathroom window before I used the hair spray, and saw the pool which had been uncovered. Frank was as good as his word. As if I were speaking to an old friend, I said, "Amanda, Lovejoy is letting us keep your pool." And then I slammed the window shut and took one last look at myself in the mirror. My face was pinched up tightly, and the expression in my eyes worried me, because, I looked worried.

*****

Lovejoy took me to dinner at a steak house instead of the Club, where he asked me thoughtfully, "Do you need both butter and sour cream on your baked potato?

"I don't even need the potato," I declared softly. "When there's a salad. I never used to eat potatoes."

"Blame me," he said, while telling the waitress "to hold her potato" but to bring him one with only butter. He patted his midriff and said, "I'm a growing boy. By the way, I've made a donation to Missions, the Tender Mercies fund. They needed money, and we had more than we needed with the sale of the house. We can't be hoarders."

He waited for me to say something. I didn't.

He tore a roll apart and took a small bite. "Giving it away made me glad. I'm so happy. We have so much. It would be a sin not to share it."

The food arrived. I didn't look up. I chewed thoughtfully, sipping the one glass of wine he had ordered for dinner instead of a whole bottle to share.

We went home, taking the slow route. At the door he unlocked it and entered first, forgetting I was just behind him. "All clear," he said, when he remembered.

I stepped back while he pressed the numbers of the security code that shut off and then restarted the security alarm.

It was a strange moment in time for me. When I lived alone in my parents' home I had known the security code and tapped the buttons coming and going. Now Lovejoy was in charge of keeping burglars out. But how was I going to keep myself safe from him? It was a question I should have asked much sooner.

While he slept, I lived with the question, reliving the moments until this moment. My chest hurt, and I wondered whether I was having a heart attack. Placing my right palm over my beating heart I felt it pounding, pounding, and every few pulses it stopped—missing a beat. I knew then that I wasn't dying of a heart attack.

My heart was breaking, and that is a much different problem. I didn't have a solution, and there was no security code to know and tap that could keep me safe now.

****

The next day over my first cup of lukewarm coffee, Frank asked, "Have you made any progress on getting your passport yet?"

I shook my head, stalling by taking a sip of coffee. The sleepless night had left a dark cloud over me. Was I imagining trouble? I had no one to ask. Amanda and Darla were both dead. I stifled an involuntary shudder.

He eyed me quizzically but pressed on with his agenda. "Next spring will be here before you know it. It's never too soon to start getting prepared. Why don't you try to get your picture made today and at least pick up the passport application forms from the post office?"

"Do we have to go on that mission trip?"

"I am inviting you to go to Athens, one of the great destinations in the world. We will still be on our honeymoon. Why wouldn't you want to go and see the world, meet strangers, see new sights? Being comfortable at home is highly over-rated."

I spoke without thinking. "I think those mission trips are busywork—romantic idylls designed to recruit people to believe they have a religious calling when they are more probably running away from their stale lives to what feels like greener pastures. I'm not unhappy or dissatisfied with my life." It was the kind of comment I used to make on the Tender Mercies committee that often put me in the dog house with the committee chairman.

Lovejoy pressed one finger against my lips and whispered, "I know what you think, but I think differently. I want to go. You're my wife. I want to come back to my room each night and find you waiting for me. Why not forget your old opinions and take a risk on living? Just say yes."

In that moment looking into his eyes and surrounded by the experience of him and fueled by my desire for him I said the only word I knew how to say to Lovejoy, "Yes."

My answer pleased him, and just that quick, I was irritated with myself for being so easy. *Who had I become?* So, I asked him, my voice querulous, "How many mission trips have you been on?"

"What did you say?" he asked. His thoughts had gone to some other place, and he hadn't heard me.

"How many mission trips have you been on?" I asked.

There were a great many questions I should have asked this man before I married him. I was only now beginning to even think of them.

He held my gaze, his attention focused. He answered as if surprised to be saying the words himself. There was a slight chuckle behind the answer—a chuckle that amused him more than it amused me. "My whole life is a mission trip," he said.

I thought he was making a joke, but he wasn't laughing. His eyes weren't either. I stared but had nothing to say.

"You might need to get a traveling haircut for Athens," he urged, adding, "Get yourself a modern haircut, Gigi. There's something about Southern women and hair that simply doesn't make sense. And if you're going to use the pool, you don't want to be fixing your hair every day. Not everyone can live in Nashville and sing on the Grand Ole Opry."

"You don't like my hair," I said, automatically patting it. I was having a very good hair day. It was still puffy and shiny from yesterday's late styling.

He shook his head tiredly and said, "You have very pretty hair, but you don't want to be packing electric rollers or that ironing thing you use to take to Athens. No one fools with their hair on a mission trip."

I think he also said, 'They don't use hairspray either,' but I wasn't sure.

Lovejoy

After Frank left, I wondered if other husbands told their wives how to do their hair and why did Lovejoy take such an interest in mine? Absentmindedly, I ran my fingers through my pretty hair and wondered irritably why he thought my hair was any of his business. A minute later I said after he had left, "I'll wear my hair any way I want to wear it."

It wasn't a prayer. It was a declaration of independence. But that didn't stop me wondering where Frank was, what my husband was doing, and as the day progressed, I just wanted Lovejoy to come home.

8

THINKING OF YOU

There's a lot to do even months before you can go on a mission trip and that's not counting the holidays. There is Christmas, New Year's, Valentine's and then, while everyone is feeling the afterglow of so much love being expressed, the church sends out letters asking for money even though Lovejoy and I were paying for ourselves. When I tried to explain to him that I didn't want my name in a money solicitation letter like the long-winded ones that the church sends out to the whole congregation, he told me not to think about it. "Just leave it to the men in charge. We've been running the church and organizing mission trips longer than you have been alive, and there's a small chance—a very small chance—that we know what we're doing."

That didn't stop me from explaining my objection. "You're using the friendships in the church to get people to send in money because they like someone and because a lot of people don't want to go on a mission trip and so they send in a check to relieve their guilt."

"Is that really how you see it?" Lovejoy asked, tilting his head thoughtfully. The light landed on him just so. I wanted to grab a simple #4 pencil and catch the way he looked—the shadows, the planes. His smile. The glint in his eyes.

Instead of drawing him, I nodded succinctly. "A lot of people do that."

"Have you ever contributed money because a friend of yours was going on a trip and you wanted to be a part of the trip by helping to pay for it?"

"Yes," I said. "I do that the same way I give graduation gifts and wedding gifts."

"Well, Darlin', if you have given money to the church for whatever your motivation was why can't you just live and let live? Other people see giving their way. You see giving your way. As long as people go to the field, why do you have to offer your opinion about it?"

It was a blunt question that shut me up. He kissed me lightly on the lips to seal the moment, but the kiss didn't work.

"Because this time it is my name being put into a churchwide solicitation letter, and I don't want people to feel that they have to prove anything by sending in a check to support me," I said.

Frank took a deep breath. "You're just afraid no one will send in a check for you because you're not very popular at church." His eyes were kind when he spoke, but those words stabbed me right in the heart. The heart!

I suffered a sharp intake of breath and replied softly—I could barely hear myself reply, "You don't know that for sure."

He put both arms around me. "I love you, Gigi, no matter how other people feel about you."

I stiffened inside his embrace until I understood that he wasn't going to let go until I relaxed and pretended I liked it. So, I did, but I was gritting my teeth while he whispered in my ear. "Just let me worry about these things. You get your hair cut, and start thinking about which clothes you will pack that you don't mind leaving behind."

"What?" I asked, pulling away.

"Oh, sure. You don't know that. We always leave behind most of our belongings. We keep our underthings. The refugees need clothes, and so we always just leave our street clothes behind for them. Pack what you don't mind leaving."

"I will need to buy some new clothes to leave behind," I said. "All of my regular clothes are pretty old."

"Girls like to shop," he said with a grin. "Buy what you want. Buy anything. Pretend you are a flower in the field that Solomon would envy."

"Huh?"

"Just an idea," he said. "Go shopping, and by the way, a lot of wives would love to hear their husbands say that."

A lot of wives don't need permission from their husbands to spend their own money on clothes for a trip that is already costing an arm and a leg. I bit my tongue this time.

"Don't you have some other place you would like to be?" I asked.

This time my question startled him.

"I'm going to my study to prepare my Bible lesson on the book of Hosea," he replied stiffly. He wasn't used to being dismissed by a woman.

"I know all about it," I said. "I read the book of Hosea when I read the announcement in the church newsletter and saw where both our names were already signed up for the trip. The secretary misspelled my name in the newsletter. How hard is it to spell Cindy? She spelled it with an "i" at the end. The only proper name that should end in an "i" is Mississippi. Really. Ending a name with that tiny little letter looks weak and unfinished."

He ignored my comment, and continued his explanation about studying Hosea.

"It's a tradition. Before a mission trip we have a special class for the team members on the book of Hosea to prepare our hearts and minds for the purpose of our trip. There are a lot of rescued street women in Athens. You don't have to come to the class if you'd rather not."

I avoided answering that question, but I was thinking: 'I might not feel very well Sunday morning and need to stay home.' "You go study. I'll go shopping. Let's meet back here for dinner, and you figure out what's for supper. I'm going to be too busy shopping to cook."

My answer startled Frank, and then he looked amused at my stab at independence. As he passed me to go to his study, he slapped me gently on the behind and said. "Buy dresses. Women in Athens like dresses. I'll be in my prayer closet for a spell," he said, ruminatively.

That was a code phrase for he was going to be in his study, but when he didn't want to be disturbed, he called it his prayer closet. I was just about to tell him that the bathroom was my prayer closet, and from now on I didn't want him talking to me or watching me while I dried off and got dressed, but I didn't. I just said the words, "Prayer closet" as if I was agreeing with him. But I wasn't really. I was thinking about Amanda.

Which one of his wives had he said died in his prayer closet? Amanda. Yes, Amanda. *"That girl really loved to iron."*

I had never ironed one single shirt for Lovejoy. He took his shirts to the dry cleaner himself. They came back pressed and folded in a box, all crisp and lightly starched. You could actually smell the starch from the shirts on days when Lovejoy got warm outside, but I liked it.

As he walked away, I thought: Lovejoy does seem a little starchy just as himself.

And then I giggled to myself, a sound he heard, and turned back to see if I was laughing at him.

I kind of was.

He closed the door to his study, which he had just renamed his prayer closet, and I wondered if that is where the other Gigi had done the ironing.

Gigi is spelled with an "I" at the end. I didn't like it.

PART 2

ECHOES OF DESIRE

Remember your Creator in the days of your youth, before the days of trouble come and the years approach when you will say, "I find no pleasure in them"--and desire no longer is stirred.

A word of caution from Ecclesiastes 12

9

YOU'RE GETTING TO BE
A HABIT WITH ME

had come to understand that Lovejoy actually preferred lovemaking in the late afternoon before supper. A new routine began. I was less startled by his desire and considerably less overwhelmed by his attentions. I began to get my balance. Like other wives—and not just his— I came to know my husband's routines and rhythms. I could sense his movements, his directions, his palls, his starts, and then the whole cycle of it all that took him one place in his mind while I went to another place in mine.

It's strange where your mind can go while your body is somewhere else. *Was I two people? Could I be three?* How would being in love change me even more? It was a question that was often answered with a distracting sigh or a muffled moan.

The window curtain in my room was slightly ajar, and I watched the breeze rustling the trees and felt the heat of his flesh on mine. I was aware of myself in a way that I never had been before—not even as a kid during Phys Ed where you are made to run and leap and do pullups while someone grades your agility and speed. Now I was aware of my pulse in a different way, my weight in how it fit and shifted, my breath as a kind of punctuation of life itself. I felt my breasts rise and fall with a breathing that was not exactly natural: some part of me was saying, *breathe, breathe.* And then Lovejoy turned over, and I saw the shape of him on the bed and how much space he was taking up. It was too much! I recalled so many days and nights of my life when I had gone to sleep alone and waked up alone and that space of being alone was very appealing. Why had I ever changed that?

He always dozed briefly before coming awake with a start. Waking up for Lovejoy was always a sudden move as if in sleep he had lost track of himself and was afraid that someone had been finding out who he really was while he wasn't on guard. There were new moments now when I fought the impulse to place my hand on the small of his back and entreat him to stay, that he could trust me with his unaware moments. Why wasn't that part of a preacher's pre-marital counseling: will you love, honor, and trust one another with your unaware moments? Lovejoy had already walked over to the window once again—an exit move of his. He was peering outside.

It was still light outside, and my thoughts moved to supper. It is mostly a woman's lot in life to think about food. Just that quick, Frank wordlessly left, almost as if he didn't remember I was there. That was new. He always said something sweet before leaving, or he touched me a final time. But that afternoon Lovejoy was just all of a sudden gone, and he didn't look back.

Lovejoy

"The honeymoon is over," I said to the ceiling, and then I got up and took a shower. He found me toweling off and walked in and watched me in the steam covered mirror. I stopped in that moment and watched us both—framed there in steam, a reflection of ourselves, of one another staring puzzled at our combined reflections in the foggy glass, and our eyes met in a kind of wonder. 'How had we gotten here?'

"Where are you going?" I asked, bending down to dry the bottoms of my legs. He studied me carefully, his eyes absorbing my motions, but there was no desire. Not a bit.

"Meeting some boys over at that house they are working on for that family that didn't qualify for that program that the city tried to put together, but the mayor couldn't pull it off."

I wasn't sure what he was talking about, but there was some ministry in town that rehabbed houses for poor people. I figured that was what he meant. I didn't really care. I had learned that Lovejoy always had some kind of community project going on that he was a part of, and there was always some kind of meeting where he needed to be that I was just finding out about. Like the letters that came to him from all over the world—two or three a month—he always seemed to be connected to someone I didn't know, and his thoughts often went there. He didn't explain much, and I didn't ask because I knew what he was doing. One day when he had been gone, I went through the cancelled checks and fully half my monthly income was given to the church and a lot of it was designated for missions.

How could you complain about someone being too generous to the church? It didn't set well with me though.

"I might end up having Mexican food with the boys. Go ahead and eat supper without me. Perhaps a boiled egg and some dry toast tonight. A light night is always a good idea if one has a tendency to carry a little extra weight. You could even tidy up the silverware drawer. It could use cleaning out."

He reached around me, kissing me lightly on the corner of my mouth while his hand patted my behind. "Yes, a boiled egg," he repeated, and then without untying my robe he turned and left.

The steam had evaporated from the glass. I saw myself clearly. My hair was wet and stringy. My face was without color or makeup.

I slipped off my robe, and took a good look at myself in the mirror. I saw what he had just seen close up. Yes, it should be a light night. A boiled egg and maybe not even a piece of toast.

That was the plan of the moment. But it didn't happen. I didn't even make another plan. I just began to move without thinking, without planning, without knowing why I was going to do what I would be doing next.

I dressed hurriedly, pulling on white stretch pants and a crimson red University of Alabama t-shirt without a bra. I don't like bras, but Lovejoy insisted that no Southern woman who understands the right kind of pride would ever leave home without wearing one. Before Lovejoy I often went braless, and that evening, I reverted to my prideless ways.

I got in my car and drove to the church. I nosed up quietly, getting closer and closer to the lit-up church windows and eventually was close enough to see my husband sitting at the meeting just as he said he would be. A part of me was deeply relieved. A part of me was deeply ashamed that I had doubted him—had not even said to myself in that interior place where you truly try not to lie that I had in a small tiny unforgiveable way not exactly believed what he had told me about the guys and the Mexican food. Which part of my secret self thought that way?

Lovejoy was sitting inside one of the meeting rooms with his back to the window, his hands cutting great swaths in the air as he proved the points he was making. I loved his hands— loved how he talked with his hands. Loved the zest he had for ideas in which he believed. Yes, sitting in the car as dusk fell and the stars began to come out, I remembered that I loved Lovejoy. Watching him I almost cried with relief and pride that he was mine.

Fifteen minutes later, he came out—didn't see me parked under the shade tree in the deep shadows across the street and off he went. I almost went home. I almost said, 'Okay, he's just toodling about, or the guys are meeting over at the Mexican restaurant,' but I didn't.

The other men didn't come out. The church light stayed on, and they stayed inside. That puzzled me. From a distance, I followed him to an address in Capitol Heights near that big Baptist church I had visited once when they hosted a Lunch 'n Learn. I recalled that the food was good, but I didn't remember what I had learned. The woman who ran it was efficient and hospitable. Her name was Marcia. I liked her.

Lovejoy steered up a steep and rounded driveway and parked on the right-hand side as if he had done it before. He opened the car door and the light came on inside. He checked himself in the rearview mirror. I heard the horn sound after he locked it remotely with his keys. That sound made the front door open, and there she was: the woman who hated me for taking her Lovejoy.

Marjeen stood framed in the doorway, and just as I had heard on the grapevine, the unmarried woman who had been keeping company with my husband was holding a baby. Lovejoy stepped right through that front door without hesitation.

It was a strange and new feeling sitting there knowing my husband was inside that house with Marjeen and a baby. I had no one to call—no one to tell my questions to. I had no friend who would help me understand it. If there had been someone I could talk to I would have said this: "I'm not surprised." I said the words out loud several times, like a refrain from a song that plays in your mind, and you can't shake the tune.

Finally, I chewed my lower lip to keep from saying the words, and when I got home, I ate a bowl of Frosted Flakes with whole milk and began to straighten out the silverware drawer. That's what Lovejoy found me doing when he came home an hour later.

10

MY RESISTANCE WAS LOW

Naturally I would have asked Frank about Marjeen when the time was right, but that same evening Lovejoy grew more and more pale. By midnight he was ailing. "I'm not myself," he said. A chill took over, and he sequestered himself in the guest room bed in order to prevent me from catching whatever had caught him. I covered him with blankets, but it wasn't until I used the electric throw and turned it to high that he began to get warm.

Frank mumbled while shivering, saying incomprehensible things. I tried to hear him and felt that I was eavesdropping on a private conversation he was having with God. "Poisoned. Poisoned. Poisoned."

I didn't know what to do. It had been years since I had lived in the house with my father, and he had not gotten sick until the last week when he passed away all of a sudden from an aneurysm to the brain.   "He went fast," the doctor declared, nodding, nodding, as if that were a good thing. I had not been able to nod in reply.

Frank had gotten sick fast too. I didn't know what to do.

When his shivering eased, he said, "A Tylenol might help, but don't get too close. I think I'm catching."

I brought him Tylenol, and placed a trash can nearby in case he needed "to throw up Mexican food." He didn't know what I was talking about.

By morning, Lovejoy said he had the flu. "My resistance is low," he confided. "I know myself. I have spells when my resistance is low, and anything can happen then. I just hope you don't catch whatever I've got. I doubt you will," he added, inscrutably and with what sounded to me like bitterness.

"My resistance is fine," I reassured him, offering soup and Saltines. I felt dead inside remembering Marjeen standing in the doorway holding a baby and the lie about the Mexican food with the boys. However, I smiled a magnolia-smile (Southern women can do this all day long no matter the circumstances), and replied, my voice sweet with concern: "Darling, you just keep still and warm. This too shall pass."

He didn't have much appetite and stayed in the guest room for two days. Then he finally allowed me to coax him to the sofa in the den, where he could watch TV. But he mostly didn't watch anything that third day. While he was feverish and periodically slept, the TV played softly in the background with images of old movies flashing by while he was wearing his colorful socks with pin-striped pajamas that he changed daily because of the fever and germs.

I was doing the washing and answering the telephone when it rang; but when I answered it, the caller hung up—the number of the caller blocked. I heard Marjeen breathing on the other end of the line, and I could feel her palpable hate. I looked over at Lovejoy on the couch, sweaty and weak, and I wondered who he was and why I had married him.

Lovejoy

As his strength began to return on the fifth day, Lovejoy let the television run with the sound increased, and we watched movies for two more days. He had many favorite older movies, and one in particular that he insisted we watch called "The Las Vegas Story." He grinned and said, "It's a mighty flimsy movie. I draw that conclusion every single time I watch it. But there's a song in it by Hoagy Carmichael. Jane sings it. Doesn't Jane sing it?"

I didn't know. Jane who?

I wasn't even sure who Hoagy Carmichael was, but I heard the song later sung about love by Jane Russell who admitted she had fallen for the wrong man—her husband, or the one that got away?

Frank looked at me after she finished singing and told me, "When I met you my resistance was low too."

From that moment on I knew that Frank tied the moments of his life to old songs that he liked to hear or hum.

"Have you ever heard Hoagy sing "Star Dust"?"

I shook my head.

"Hoagy wrote it, but if you hear him sing it as he wrote it you almost won't recognize the song. I'll tell you who made that song what it is today," Lovejoy said before he drifted off to sleep. He never did tell me about "Star Dust." I didn't know the song.

The ringing telephone roused him. Again, the caller hung up. His brow furrowed. "Pollster. Telemarketer. Do we really need a land line anymore?" he mused to himself. "A lot of the boys are closing down their land lines—just using their cells. They are unplugging from cable TV too, but I don't know how that will work out. They explained it to me the other evening, but I couldn't follow what they were saying exactly. Technology doesn't belong to my generation. Something about sticks sticking into the TV and connecting to the internet. My darling, I do not think I'm going to be much help to you with this TV business and how it's changing." It was a strange apology, and inside it, I knew he meant so much more. I was afraid to ask what exactly.

"Do you want me to change the channel?" I asked, settling in beside him. We had been together for six days around the clock, and strangely, I'd missed him. I missed the comfort of him—the belonging to him. The vision of Marjeen standing in the doorway receded. *Surely, he was just telling her good-bye one more time.*

The white thermal blanket was bunched around Frank, and he needed a shower. His hair needed washing. He had bathed the day before, but he was still running a fever from time to time. Sweating gave him an uncharacteristic rumpled look.

"You are sans brassiere...." He observed, his gaze fixed now on the flashing TV screen as he scanned channels. His tone of voice was disapproving and disappointed.

I hadn't worn a bra since the night out in front of Marjeen's house. Lovejoy would soon give me a lecture on a woman's pride if I didn't. I thought I wouldn't mind hearing it again if I didn't have to wear a bra while he gave it.

His hand fell on top of my thigh where it rested. Lovejoy had a beautiful hand. It reminded me of hands on statues in museums that had been carved by people like Rodin and Michelangelo. His hand rested in a graceful cupping arc. His fingers were slender, tapered—his nails tended and not too long. Looking at them made me remember that I needed a manicure.

He seemed aware of my admiration and slid his hand closer.

"Desire. You want to be desired. I want to be desired. What you really want and what I really want is to have all of my unlovable parts loved absolutely. That's the basis of absolute desire. My desire. Your desire. God's desire. It's not our beautiful parts we want desired and loved. It's our unbeautiful parts that need the most love."

"I desire you," I said simply. It was still true. It was as true as the repeated refrain from six nights ago: *I am not surprised. I am not surprised. I am not surprised.*

How could you be in love and be in desire and still live in a state of wonder called *I am not surprised*?

"I know," he admitted, and there was fatigue in the confession. "Did you know that I have a way with the ladies?"

It was such a surprising question that I didn't know what to say.

"You have a way with me," I agreed softly. A part of me was humming inside now, and I wanted him to be well immediately and to go and take a shower and take me for a ride on the boat. I didn't have to think about Marjeen if I didn't want to. The voice inside my head that said those words sounded like a 12-year-old girl.

"Oh, my dear. I've always had a way with women. You don't know the half of it. My way with women is my strength and my weakness. It is the part of me I want you to desire, and it is the part of me I want you to forgive." He turned to me, still weak and sick, and in my view, now a penitent who was leading up to telling me the story of Marjeen standing in the doorway and his not eating Mexican food with the boys after all. "Could you forgive me anything?" he asked. His eyes searched mine for something I wasn't sure I could give.

"Yes," I said simply, in faith. It was truly the only word I knew how to say to Lovejoy. Maybe all women said yes to him as easily as I did. Knowing that didn't stop me from saying it.

"You really like boat rides under blue skies." He was not judging me—just observing.

I nodded, for I longed to go on a boat ride with him again and watch the birds and not think about fevers, the flu, or Marjeen. *Did we really need to talk about her? Couldn't we just forget it—her?* I was not surprised to feel that way. I have always been a keen sweeper of bad news under the nearest available rug.

He was here with me now. Lovejoy had picked me.

"You don't know it yet, but one day, God willing, I shall take you on the boat on an autumn day when the air is brisk— almost cold—and we shall display ourselves like children beneath the eyes of God himself, and I will show you something you have not yet imagined." He turned and held my gaze—fixed, hypnotic— "Because I know something you don't, and you have not yet even imagined it."

I closed my eyes and imagined such a moment in time ahead, and he continued, "Gigi, long ago and far away, I was on such a boat in the cold and the sun was shining. The sun was shining in the cold. I was alone but not alone and stripped down to my shorts to feel how cold it could be on a sunny day, and there in the silence of that heated cold I experienced the call of God upon my life that has shaped my future and has now claimed yours."

His hand slipped down my knee and nestled there, but he was unaware of that, I think. I took a deep breath. He was a lot better. I prayed the phone wouldn't ring.

"The water was calm—so calm, so blue, and the aloneness was something. It was something. And that's when I came to understand as the water moved beneath me and as I kept the boat steady in what soon became a light wind that I had a particular gift." He eyed me mischievously. "I have a way with the ladies. I was trying to tell you before. It's hard to explain."

I don't know what I was expecting to hear, but it wasn't that again.

"You have a way with the ladies." It wasn't news to me, but it was his idea of a self-revelation.

He nodded seriously, raising his pale hand to stroke his chin where he especially needed to shave.

"Of course, you have a way with me," I agreed. "I love you. I married you."

"You and so many others," he said with a cough that rose up in him.

I drew back and looked at him. He was sweating again. There was a bead of sweat trailing down the side of his face, and he was flushed. His fever which had abated was spiking again. I was about to offer him some more Tylenol, when he said: "All ladies are the same really. You want to be desired—to be distracted from self-consciousness and guilt not so much over being sinful but for somehow needing to be desired makes you feel guilty. I take that away. With due diligence I give you that—prepare a pathway for you to find something bigger than me. But I give you me at first. It is my spiritual gift to you," he shrugged. "God made me this way, and women like me."

"You have a way with the ladies," I repeated dully. Visions of women crawling over other people in the pews to sit beside him came to mind. Visions of women flanking both sides of him at church resurfaced without my trying to think about it. A vision appeared of Marjeen hearing the horn sound and flinging open the door, standing there welcoming him in the doorway. Images rose up of that first day in the car when he declared himself and kissed me. Had been kissing me ever since. All the images coalesced, layered with feelings and now a new and undeniable suspicion.

"I only wish I had learned to play the piano, too," he said with real feeling.

And then my husband drifted off to sleep with his hand where it rested and me beside him wondering which one of us would die first.

11

ALL THE WAY

"I have an assignment for you. A good work to do," Frank announced gently, leaning across the breakfast table to tap my hand. He did that sometimes, applying a subtle pressure I could not ignore with one of his beautiful hands. For even though perspective and reason had invaded my understanding of our relationship, I found myself fascinated by his touch. His beautiful hands. I had come alive in a new way to his beautiful hands while he had the flu; and after he had finally gotten rid of the fever completely, he teased me about my admiration of that part of himself.

"It took you a while to see my hands. Oh, you thought you had seen them, but then you really saw them. And now you can't stop seeing them. You are funny that way. You women look at one thing and then another thing like little hummingbirds going from flower to flower looking for nectar, and you're never really satisfied for long." His eyes and voice were laced with amusement, and it was difficult to get angry with him when he said things like that because he was so beautiful.

There were times when I wanted to turn to somebody and say, "Isn't he the most beautiful man you've ever seen?" Do other wives think that about their husbands? Did Jane Russell ever sing a song like that?

I looked down at his hand, that one finger, and just that quick, I didn't like the way he knew how to use his beauty to bully me. "We are already going on a mission trip that will cost us an arm and a leg. What else do you want me to do?"

He sighed. "You do not need to worry about the mission trip. By the time it happens, you'll be ready. But I do have a responsible role to fulfill at church, and you are my wife. It is my duty to support and encourage the work of others, especially missions, and the best way to do that is to help people participate. It means so much to our missions' director to have people take an interest in his mission trips and the annual Missions Conference. That's what I want you to do— take an interest. Show that interest by doing something."

"I'll do something if it will make you happy. Otherwise, I wouldn't be thinking about this at all for all kinds of reasons you never asked me about and which I've never told you."

I waited for Frank to ask me about my reasons, but he didn't.

That is true of many men and often true of Lovejoy. You offer them a small hook to bait their curiosity about what you are thinking, and they don't take it. I kept my thoughts to myself, but I didn't want to help with missions—and not being asked my reasons was one of the reasons.

Lovejoy dismissed my comment with a wave of his beautiful hand and continued, his voice growing softer as it always did when he was serious about persuading me to do something I didn't want to do.

Lovejoy

"It's just a simple act of tender mercy on your part. You believe in mercy, don't you?" His question probed me.

He didn't wait for me to reply, but continued: "The Missions Conference is coming, and we need a Bible verse to use as our slogan."

"Does it have to be a Bible verse?" I asked, raring back in the kitchen chair. The wooden spokes were hard against my back, and I resolved to buy cushions for them. After the sale of my house Lovejoy had donated my dining room set with cushioned chairs to the shelter for homeless people to be sold at their thrift store. I missed my cushioned chairs and my own dining table. I looked at him irritably.

He stifled a response of impatience, collected himself, and pressed on my hand with one finger: "Of course it has to be a Bible verse. We are a Bible-reading church. The Bible is the inspiration of truth, the only tool for faith and practice."

"I've heard the preacher say something like that," I replied. "It's just I wonder about big truths being distilled into little sentences, and I have seen people use little Bible verses to prove a point that was beside the point. Besides, Mark Twain and Ben Franklin made some great quotes. Couldn't we just choose one of them? They are easy to find. I've got a book of famous quotes in a box somewhere if you didn't donate it to the thrift store." I knew Lovejoy wouldn't like the idea. I knew that none of those quotes would work, but I said it anyway because he didn't take my bait earlier and ask me my reasons for not blindly supporting his missions.

"That's people. Franklin and Twain. That's not the Bible. I realize that you think differently about these matters, but the missions guy needs a Bible verse, and he needs someone from the congregation to contribute it in order to feel encouraged about his work," Lovejoy said, settling back in his chair. He didn't look uncomfortable. That irritated me.

We needed cushions for these chairs. My chairs from my house had had cushions. Why hadn't we donated his— Amanda's-- set to the shelter and their thrift store and kept my table and chairs with the cushions?

"Why?" I asked, reasonably. And that one word stood for a lot of questions growing in my mind about the choices Lovejoy had made with my possessions and money since we had shifted from first desire to this next place in marriage— not altogether past desire but, well, his hands were beautiful but I could resist them, and they could make me irritable. He was oblivious to what I was thinking.

"Leadership attracts participation, and if people aren't participating, then JD isn't really leading."

Should I care? I didn't say those words. I said these: "If JD comes up with the verse, it's a dictatorship, not a democracy."

"I wish sometimes you would listen to yourself. You say things very harshly." He winced, remembering an earlier discussion we had had about preachers and, well, missionaries whom I called Gigolos for Jesus. What else do you call someone who is nice to you in the name of Jesus because his job description calls for it and he gets paid to be nice?

"I'm sorry," I replied, withdrawing my hand. But really, a lot of God-fearing men expected lonely women in the church to be their benefactors. I couldn't help it if the phrase Gigolos for Jesus played in my head.

Lovejoy

He retracted his as well and settled back in the chair, crossing his legs. He was wearing his lemon-yellow socks. They were thin and cool, made of a silk combination. He had confessed his penchant for good and colorful socks. "The finer things should be appreciated, and I appreciate really fine socks."

At night wearing slippers imported from a British men's store, Lovejoy rinsed out his silk-blend socks in his bathroom sink with cold lavender scented water only and draped them over the towel bar in his walk-in shower.

I offered to wash his socks for him, but he said, no.

"Don't turn yourself into a washerwoman for me. You are my lover," he said.

"I like being your…. Mrs. Lovejoy," I said, tasting the name. I liked the title more than his word, lover.

He nodded briefly, turning his gaze toward the door. He wanted to be somewhere else, I saw, and I didn't stop him with more conversation. He didn't leave immediately, however. Instead, he finished the conversation he had begun. "If you would just thumb through the Bible and try to identify three or four verses that are short and would inspire attendance and interest in the Missions Conference that would be very helpful. If you won't do it just because you are a member of the congregation, do it for me," he said. "If you don't know how to start, go to the index at the back of your Bible and read some key words. Maybe something will click with you."

"Is this your idea of a trophy wife?" I whispered.

He didn't seem to hear me. I was glad and also disappointed. I kind of wanted an argument—to tussle with him-- and I can't really explain that.

Frank stood up, slowly, and then walked around the table, and using the same forefinger he traced the outline of my jaw. His finger moved naming the features of me that belonged to him, and I closed my eyes. He stopped at my mouth, outlining the shape of my mouth and stopped at last by laying his finger against my lips. Instinctively, he pressed again. Leaning over he whispered in my ear words that he had never said before, "We are judged by our words. Be careful with yours." He kissed my cheek, a chaste and brotherly kiss.

I was disappointed and lingered with my eyes closed, waiting for him to correct his mistake.

"I'm going out," he said instead.

I didn't ask him where. He didn't like to tell me where he was going. Men are like that. I've heard that explanation in various ladies' rooms my whole life. Men don't like to explain where they are going. They don't like to talk about their feelings. Men don't like for women to say too many words to them at one time. Men don't like casseroles. Men like meat and potatoes. Men don't like for women to make scenes so when they have bad news to deliver, they take them to restaurants where they will keep quiet. I've heard that and a whole lot more from wives about their husbands in the ladies' lounge.

Lovejoy stopped in the doorway and said, "Don't just sit on the couch and stare out the window watching for me to return. I can feel you waiting for me and watching. Live your life, too," he advised. "If I'd known that you would fall so hard...." He didn't finish his thought, but looked at me thoughtfully, mournfully, and then with resolve, he left.

I moved to the window and adjusted the dusty white mini blinds so that there was barely a view of the driveway or the street. Then, I sat down on the couch just as he predicted I would and relived the feel of his finger on my hand, pressing down and how he had outlined my face, creating me with his touch. I relived the feel of his breath in my hair; and in spite of what he said, I sat on the couch waiting for him, listening. From time to time, I got up and changed the loads in the laundry and wiped down the kitchen counters and made the beds, but that doesn't take as much time as you believe it does when you tell the story of housekeeping to someone else and want to make the work sound hard. So hard!

When Frank's car turned the corner hours later, I knew he was home and even though I had been waiting for him, I got moving. I hurried into the kitchen and began to bring pans out of the cabinet and place them on the stove as if I were about to cook so he wouldn't know that I had mostly just been waiting for him to come home.

"What's for supper?" he asked, materializing in the doorway. He looked tired and windblown. His shoes were dirty, and he would be washing his socks very soon. I walked over to him and buried my face against his chest. He smelled differently—of beer and air freshener. Lemongrass.

He pushed me gently away. "Need a shower, Geeg. Did you find us a Bible verse for the Missions Conference?"

I hadn't remembered at all and shook my head, disappointing him.

And then he knew that in spite of his warning and his request I had done just what he had asked me not to do: waited for him.

He looked troubled but turned the conversation to dinner. "What's for supper?"

"Baked fish cakes and little green peas," I replied instantly.

"Do you have your heart set on that meal?" he asked, looking over at the oven which was still pre-heating. I had just turned it on when he pulled into the driveway.

"Let's go to the Country Club. Why don't you freshen up? I'll shower and change, and we'll go out and have a night on the town. I'll get you home by eight for your show."

It was just five o'clock. We would be at the Club by six and home by seven thirty. We would be sitting in our respective chairs by eight after brushing our teeth in separate bathrooms. He wouldn't put on his pajamas until he closed his door behind him. He locked his door. I didn't.

"The peas are still in the freezer with the fish cakes."

"I surmised as much," he remarked.

He wanted to say something else but thought better of it. I hurried to dress, glad to be going out and miffed that he hadn't asked me earlier in the day. I could have spent more time dressing and not just waiting.

1 2

MORE THAN YOU KNOW

We went to dinner at the Club. The truth is, you are supposed to meet a spending minimum each month as part of your membership agreement, and so Frank ordered a whole bottle of wine for twenty-eight dollars. That gave me a great appetite, so I said yes to filet mignon and a loaded baked potato. Under the table Frank's foot toyed with mine occasionally, and his eyes twinkled, amused. Alfred wasn't working. A young man we had never met was, and he lacked the companionable enthusiasm that Lovejoy likes when he is having a special meal out and expects the waiter to be a third mostly silent member of whatever celebration he imagines we are having.

I didn't know what Lovejoy had in mind, but I was glad for the wine and willing to overlook the fact that the server didn't know they were out of filet mignon so we had to settle for sirloin!, that bread pudding wasn't served until next Sunday, that when guests finish a salad you take away the plate, and that when the bread bowl is empty you bring more. Lovejoy rarely shows impatience, but he was displeased when the bread bowl stayed empty and when he asked that more rolls be brought, ten minutes passed and the rolls were not warm when they finally were delivered.

It was nothing to me. It mattered to him. I drank a second glass of wine and ate slowly.

You can be sitting across from your husband having a dinner, enjoying the food, and looking forward to whatever might happen next and also be simultaneously very annoyed with him.

After dessert of lemon meringue pie with toasted almonds and small demitasse cups of decaffeinated espresso, Lovejoy said, "I need to talk with you about Marjeen."

"Who?" I asked, growing numb. I had tried to repress knowing my husband had been to see her—another woman-- that one time before he had the flu. I had decided that Marjeen was pestering him. She couldn't let go, and he was still trying to convince her that he had married someone else: his lover. Me. I am Mrs. Lovejoy.

"Marjeen from church," he said quietly. "You've seen her around—probably seen her in the ladies' room, I suspect. Marjeen has a baby now."

"Did she get married?" The question just flew out of my mouth.

He reached across the table and covered my hand with his. "Try to hear this without being afraid or insecure. I have made the prayerful decision that the baby and Marjeen are my responsibility. I need—I want-- to write her a check, and it needs to be on the house account that has both our names so that she knows that you know. When she knows you know, there will be nothing she can say to make this unfortunate situation worse. Believe me, women can make a bad situation worse—so much worse than it ever needs to be."

"Marjeen has a baby now, and you are responsible."

Fatigue filled his gaze and deepened his voice. He spoke plainly. "Yes. I do not wish to discuss the details of my life that happened before you and I married, but yes. I take responsibility for Marjeen and her baby. I am hoping you will be able to simply accept that—let's not have a scene here in the Country Club."

"You hope that I can accept your responsibility for Marjeen and the baby," I repeated.

"Evidently she has always wanted a baby," he said dismissively. And then he looked at me as if suddenly thinking of a question he should have asked, "Cindy, did you ever want children?"

I did not allow myself to think about children as I did not allow myself to think about anything I couldn't reasonably have. I blotted my mouth on the napkin so that he couldn't see my lips were trembling.

He signaled for the check, scribbled his name with a flourish, and we left the dining room in sober silence. I had not made a scene.

When we were in the car, I said woodenly, broken in ways I didn't know you could be, "You were right to tell me. Give Marjeen what she needs."

"Christian mercy," he said. "Whether she's wrong or right, in or out of wedlock, the child needs care, and she sought help from me. I have taken responsibility for her and the child."

I knew then that my husband was practicing how he would explain that gift of money to anyone else if he was ever asked to, and I stored the words in case I needed to repeat them after him again to a lawyer. And then I recalled the pre-nup. And…. we had been spending my money, not his. If we divorced, he would take his money with him, and I would take what was left of mine. I no longer had a house. "Because you are responsible. You are responsible," I said the words with wonder and the beginning of a heartbreak I had never known existed before that moment.

"Marjeen is like a daughter to me," he explained carefully. His voice grew softer, and I had to lean forward to hear him.

"She may be my daughter. Her mother says she is. Her mother was an unfortunate woebegone creature who needed love. Her mother's situation was so desperate I had to help her once upon a time. I wasn't married when I knew her. Life happens. And now life has happened again, and I must help— I want to help-- Marjeen." His voice grew stiff with formality and a defensiveness I had not heard before. "Marjeen and I were just becoming acquainted—as we should be—when I decided to court you."

"As you want to be," I repeated dully.

He looked at me with a strange kindness in his eyes. "Life happens, and it can be awfully messy. Don't let the mess distract you. Focus on the obvious answer. Tender mercy."

"Life happens?"

"It's a glorious idea, if you will let yourself think about it. Imagine! Life happens."

"It happens for a reason," I replied softly. He didn't hear me—just continued talking about Marjeen's mother. He didn't call her woebegone again. I expected him to use that word again, but he didn't. He used other words. I almost heard them. He was speaking from the other end of a tunnel, but it was really just the other side of the front seat of a car and we were in it going somewhere called home. I wondered who he was and why we were in a car together going anywhere but especially a place called home.

"Marjeen's mother didn't have much education and no well-to-do aunts and uncles and parents like you had to leave you provided for. Who knows what would have happened to you if you hadn't inherited the money you enjoy today?"

And as if he had said nothing terribly important, Frank continued musing about what he considered my failings rather than his own: "I have never understood your objection to the Tender Mercies fund helping people out of work or out of luck. You didn't earn anything you have, and you judge other people meanly for having less than you do."

That sentence hung in the air as he parked my car in the driveway. He had begun to drive my car because the air conditioner in his Buick no longer worked. It is too expensive to repair," he said. "When the air conditioner dies, you might as well just buy a new car," he said, with resignation. "And in the South, you must have an air-conditioned car."

Only he hadn't bought a new car yet. He was driving mine. And he was about to write a check to Marjeen on the house account.

When he turned off the car, we both let ourselves out. I was surprised my legs could work. When I really needed physical help getting out of the car, my husband didn't know it and he didn't give it. I couldn't remember when he had stopped helping me in and out of the car. Our relationship had not begun that way.

As we reached the front door Frank unlocked it quietly and when we entered, I said, "We need cushions for the dinette chairs. They're getting harder and harder to sit on."

13

BLUES IN THE NIGHT

After the conversation about Marjeen, Lovejoy slept in what we didn't call anything except the other bedroom. It was never the guest room or the spare room. It was just the other room, and Lovejoy began to sleep there without explaining himself. There were feelings in me for which I had no reference—couldn't explain or name, but there was a kind of rage that drove them. And guilt. Frank had confessed to something true about Marjeen; and having listened to him, I was the one who felt guilty. I was at a loss for why I felt this way, and I couldn't sleep.

I got up, and sans robe, sans slippers, sans answers I went to that other room where he was snoring gently. No problem sleeping for him! I twisted the knob. It was locked. The door was locked. The door was locked. The door was locked. Really?

It was his locked bedroom door that finally caused me to create a ruckus. I had not planned to do it. I didn't mean to make a scene. But we weren't in a restaurant, and no one was watching or listening, so I started beating on his door with my right fist. When he finally, tiredly, opened the door, I didn't ask him what I had planned to say but blew up with this question instead: "Why did you really marry me?"

The sound of my voice was loud—too loud for the hallway or the other room, and in its way, bullying, pathetic, and sadly, petulant. I was too old to be petulant and too much of a Southern lady to want to be seen as a bully, but standing in the doorway looking at this man who was my husband I thought I had a right to finally ask and receive answers to my question: "Why did you really marry me?"

His voice was sorrowful and patient, his eyes kind with a determined tolerance I had not seen before. In spite of my anger, I was moved by the searching tenderness in his gaze. I didn't know it then, but I would remember that expression of tenderness in his eyes for the rest of my life.

And then he spoke, this man who had wooed me with his early "Amens" and now was using his voice for crisis management.

"Why all of a sudden are you demanding to know *that*?" He asked with an air of polite detachment, as if Marjeen hadn't happened. "Why is it not enough to know that I love you? If something happened with another woman before I ever met you, what is that to you? Really?" he asked, stepping past me out of the other room. He moved gently past me through the hallway, leaving me behind and positioned himself on a chair in the living room.

Reluctantly I followed him. He sat composed, graceful, his features sharp with a maturity of age that looked good on him. I was shocked in that moment that he could literally take my breath away. He seemed to know this, and rather than draw back—become smug or powerful in his knowledge of my weakness for him, he sighed as if he thought my desire was an impediment in the moment—a problem between us. Maybe it was.

I closed my eyes briefly to blot out the sight of him. Desire eased. When I opened them again, he had turned off the light, believing I suppose that the lamp was too bright for me, but it wasn't. He was too much for me. No woman in the ladies' room had ever made that confession. Was I the only wife who felt this way about her husband?

"Tell me why you married me," I entreated, my voice breaking. "Because if you don't tell me, I will imagine the worst."

"What is the worst?" he asked calmly, waiting for me to come closer. I didn't.

He studied the floor, considering his options. He took his time, rising slowly. And first I thought he was being theatrical, and then I realized he was stiff. He had come right from bed and was now moving slowly as fast as he could but slowly. I took deep breaths while he made his way to me.

That didn't stop me from saying what I had been trying to not even think. "You could have married me because you didn't want to grow old by yourself. You could have married me because you thought you might need a caregiver. You could have married me for...." and I hesitated to say this because I couldn't take it back, "for my money." And then I said, with a kind of wonder and remorse, "But I wasn't rich. I only had enough."

"That's one of the things I liked about you at first," he said, smiling wryly. "You were satisfied with so little, and I wanted you to enjoy more about being alive than you were doing. You woke up to mimosas and bread pudding. When we went for a drive, all the colors around us passed through you, and I saw that your heart was like a magnolia bud ready to blossom and I thought you were...."

"Were what?" I demanded.

"Not like other women," he said, with remembered wonder in his voice. "I thought you were not like other women, and I was ready for a change. The money? It's just a tool. Just a commodity to be traded. That's all money is."

What he said to me didn't feel like a compliment. My feelings were hurt, I was tired, and I let my temper explode, finally. "You've certainly been giving my commodity away pretty freely. You traded it to be a big man at church."

He grew ashen with that statement, growing cold right in front of me. I thought he might shrivel up and die, but that didn't stop me from saying what was really on my mind. "This business with Marjeen.... it's not setting well with me. Not at all."

Lovejoy studied me, and while he did, I studied him. We breathed in tandem, calculating if we had gone too far or not far enough. I saw him collect himself, become resolute. And his composure angered me.

He managed a certain debonair indolent grace associated with old movie actors like Cary Grant. Even furious and exasperated with him, I liked his looks, the shape of his mouth, the way his eyes opened wider when he was about to speak, the slant of his jaw, the hairline still marked and strong. In that moment his mouth trembled slightly, however. From time to time, so did his beautiful hands. I had caught glimpses of this sudden tremor that would from time to time move through him. It was like an earthquake that happened on the other side of the world, but the last little ripple of it showed up in him every now and again. Not often. It didn't alarm me. He never mentioned it. He had learned to position himself to still and disguise the trembling, but it occurred. *Why did men not want you to see them weak?*

"My very dear girl. It's almost impossible to answer your questions. If you don't trust me enough that you have to ask the question you won't trust the answer either." His response was simple, reasonable, and maddening.

I felt each word land. Word by word, I experienced a new sensation inside of me that came to life in that very moment: less desire for him. It scared me. Even though I had fought the overwhelming sensation of my desire for him, I was not prepared to give it up—to go back to my numb unfeeling self which had moved through life before Lovejoy. Before Lovejoy. Before Lovejoy. I didn't want to imagine life after desire, after Lovejoy. I tried to stop that from happening by paying attention to it: *Don't let go of the desire altogether, because when that's gone, what's left?* But even reason did not stop me from letting it go. I felt the desire drain out of me just as I was noting his mouth, the upward curl of his lips that hinted at laughter and passion. I recalled the depths of a kiss that had caused me to wake up to myself and the world. No matter what his explanation could have been for marrying me, I felt that it had to include the word *victim*.

It was a rude awakening. An awakening to a new kind of numbness, maybe a new kind of death. The more Lovejoy talked, the less desire I felt for him. And if he kept talking, by the end of whatever he could say I feared there would be no desire left at all between us. I was afraid of that happening. I wasn't sure what existed purely between us without desire. What did either of us mean when we said, "I love you"? Inexplicably my mind flitted to the image of the old house he had shown me on the first Sunday drive and how a photographer had been keeping a record of the changes made with the passing of time by taking snapshots. What would anyone learn from doing that?

"Why do you wear silk socks in funny colors?" I asked.

He looked down at his feet, considering. Then he looked up, his blue eyes paler now, and there was a new weakness in them that wasn't there just seconds before. Not yesterday. Not the day before. Not a minute before. Lovejoy was growing weaker right in front of me. I had the oddest notion that I was the cause that was making him sick. We were living in the house that Faulkner built, and I was Emily. *Was I Emily? A rose by any other name—even Gigi—is what? Poison?*

His voice was filled with wonder when he replied, as if he were just learning it himself: "We always keep a little something of ourselves back for ourselves. You do that too. There are days when I think I've never met the real you. I keep waiting for the girl I thought I was marrying to come out and join me—to trust me enough to come out from where you hide and stay. You visit from time to time, but you don't stay."

He looked at me wonderingly and with a kind of sober grief.

I waved aside his slowly delivered comments.

"Do you love me? I demanded. It was a foolish question— an unnecessary question. I was a child having a temper tantrum. I knew it, but I couldn't stop.

A strange sadness passed over his face. "We have been married a while now, and you ask that question?"

"You haven't answered it."

"That's because what you may mean by love is obviously not what I mean by love, but my answer is, yes. Believe me or not," he said tiredly. "I love you as much as any man can love any woman."

The words were delivered with a kind of sad finality that caused my chest to hurt.

Then without touching me at all, Lovejoy walked down the hallway toward what was now without discussion his private bedroom and didn't look back. The door closed, but he didn't lock it. He didn't need to do it. The defeated expression on his face and the resigned tone of his voice locked me out.

For the first time since we married, I didn't feel compelled to go after him, to stand outside his closed door wondering about him inside and why he kept himself apart from me, ever. Standing on the other side of his closed door I whispered to him: "You are the one who doesn't come out. I'm right here, waiting."

I went outside to the back porch and inhaled deeply, trying to catch my breath. It had grown ragged and short. I couldn't breathe. My gown was sticky with perspiration and too hot. I peeled it off, dropping it on the cement sidewalk that encircled the pool. The moon was reflected in the water of the swimming pool which was dark and kind of scary. I raised a hand and massaged my neck, which felt sore with suspicion. My breasts felt limp with age and loss. My legs didn't want to hold me up, but I didn't want to go back in the house. I could feel him in there, passing away from something about me that was making him ill, and I didn't know what it was.

The fence that encircled our yard was intact and the gate was locked. Amanda's swimming pool had been recently cleaned, the water treated, the filter checked.

I looked up at an overhanging tree limb and saw the deep purple sky—waited for a bird, any bird—to fly by, but I was alone in the fenced backyard under the limb and the canopy of evening sky. The sliding doors that led inside to the den seemed more like a gate for a cage than a door for a house.

I walked to the edge of the pool and put my foot on the first of three steps that led down into the shallow end of the pool. The water was cool, clean. I moved down another step, sitting on the next one in my panties and nothing else. My fingers reached out and played with the surface of the water, touching the reflections of starlight and finding leaves instead. I eased my way down to the last step in the shallow end of the pool and sat down, finding the bottom with my hands. The water was around my breasts, which became more buoyant but were still in ways that are difficult to admit, lifeless, limp, a burden. I pushed forward with a breast stroke, moving into the water and underneath the moon and starlight and made my way to the deep end of the pool. There I treaded water for a little while until I grew tired. Then I turned over on my back and floated, letting myself become one with the water and in ways that it had never happened before with the night and the starlight, and the moonlight and the breeze until all that was left of me—or so it seemed—was the air coming from my body in deep wordless sighs that joined the atmosphere and became part of the energy that seemed to surround me.

"You all right out there?" his voice called to me, ending the peace.

I don't know how many times my very responsible, twice bereaved husband called out. The question arrived as an echo, as if it had been said some minutes before and finally made its way through the atmosphere to reach me.

"Honey?"

"Sweetheart?"

"Don't be like that."

The words and the questions reached me while my hands were fluttering underneath me, creating the buoyance I needed to stay afloat.

"Gigi," he called. And he sounded scared. His voice moved me.

I turned over and swam back to the side of the pool where he was standing, holding my robe. Gripping the side of the pool, I looked up at him.

He stooped down closer and said, "Don't you think it's time you came inside?"

I answered by flipping on my back and swimming away from him.

I could feel his body stiffen, and spitting water as I swam backwards away from him, I saw him turn, look disoriented, shake his head. He didn't know what to do. I was getting away from him.

He couldn't see me in the dark, and I said, "Good."

He went back in the house, and I said the word again.

"Good."

But he was not inside long.

He came back out with a bottle of wine and two glasses. He placed them on the small wrought iron table between two lounge chairs and filled them. Then he sat back, reclining and began to sip his wine.

My skin was growing pickled, my body tired from swimming and floating. I thought I had escaped him; but there he was, waiting for me in the dark.

There was no other exit. I swam to the steps in the shallow end and climbed out, retrieving my robe which he had dropped on the concrete sidewalk that encircled the pool.

I slipped into it and walked to where he was sitting.

"You have made your case for keeping the pool."

"I've always enjoyed swimming. I just don't like to do it in a crowd because I don't like the way I look in a swimsuit."

"You have apparently solved that dilemma," he said, referring to my swimming mostly nude covered in moonlight, starlight, and a pair of clingy wet diaphanous panties.

"Yes," I said with satisfaction. "I have solved that problem." And then I took a long sip of my wine and stared at the sky. The moon had moved behind a bank of clouds and the breeze had stilled. No birds sang in the nighttime. The silence was mysterious and inviting.

"Do you have any more responsibilities I need to know about?" I asked quietly, but he heard me.

"I have many secrets that if you knew them would make you uneasy because you are so naive," he replied. "But I have no more responsibilities that should impact your little, little…." He didn't finish his thought.

I turned over on the chaise to face him. "Tell me one secret."

He took three long breaths before answering. "You will never have strength enough to leave me," he predicted quietly.

I looked at him to see if he was making a boast or a command. He wasn't. He was only telling the truth as far as he knew it.

"If you have no more responsibilities—no other women with claims on you--why would I want to leave you?"

Lovejoy took a sip of his wine and replied, "Why indeed. Women get in such a ruffle about things. Are you hungry?"

I was hungry. Very hungry. I hadn't eaten much supper, and the swim had given me an appetite.

"You stay out here and sip some more of your wine, and I'll do a little something in the kitchen. A little snack."

He rose, moving behind me. He leaned over and placed his hand on my right shoulder. I waited for it to move down, somewhere. But it didn't at first. Lovejoy's hand moved across my chest and to my neck where his hand cupped my throat. "You were very elegant swimming in the pool, like a swan across the water." His hand tightened, feeling my throat. I took a sip of wine and swallowed demonstratively so he could feel the movement in his hand. I didn't choke, but I had to fight the impulse.

He responded by leaning over and kissing the top of my head. "Come inside when you're ready," he invited.

He rose then, leaving the bottle behind. I drank another glass of wine before picking up my glass and going through the sliding glass French doors and into the breakfast area that extended from Amanda's kitchen.

Lovejoy was stirring soup on the stove, his back to me. "Are you hungry, my dear?"

He had already asked me that question. He was repeating himself, making conversation because he couldn't afford to say anything else.

Watching him, I was free of desire for him.

But I was hungry.

He knew I was watching him. I could feel his attention—his listening, his wondering, and there was something new present--a gentleness to his waiting that intrigued me. It was a gentleness born of his aloneness and how life was for him— what aloneness was for him. What desire had been with other women and was now with me and why he kept himself apart from me while accusing me of being the one who kept herself in reserve. Testing us both, I walked over to him and encircled my arms around him and pulled him to me wondering what he would feel like now that I was free of desire for him. "I will keep you company while you stir."

These are the promises that follow marriage vows.

His hand kept stirring the soup. "Just be a minute," he replied brightly. "You want to put something on?"

He shouldn't have said that because it gave me a tool I could use to protect myself, to be myself while still with him.

He couldn't bear for me to be naked in front of him. That was important knowledge. I could fight naked if I had to do that. I could fight him naked.

My eyes closed, my body tired, my thoughts still floating at ease like leaves upon the water's surface, I leaned my face against his back and felt his shoulder muscles stiffen. I thought about shedding the robe and eating sans clothes at the table to see how long he would be able to stand my prideless ways. First sans bra, now sans clothes altogether.

Then, knowing he wouldn't be able to stand it at all and I wasn't sure if I could even pull off such a bluff, I went to my room and tugged a large T-shirt over my head and the pair of white stretch pants he abhorred. Frank made no objection to my dining ensemble when I returned to the table set with two bowls of steaming soup.

"Buttered bread," he said, pointing out the obvious.

I tore a slice in two and took a large bite. Butter. I like butter.

Lovejoy leaned over his steaming bowl and spooned a bite of butternut squash soup into his mouth. I ate with my elbows on the table, my body relaxed and easy in my clothes while my right foot reached out under the table to find his, teasingly. When you are free of desire you can afford to be mischievous. Some people mistake that for flirtation, but really, I wasn't flirting. I was daring him.

A small smile eased the corner of his mouth and he looked up again. "I'm right here," he assured me.

"So am I," I replied.

It felt in that moment as if we had recited a different version of our wedding vows.

This stage of the honeymoon was different. Lovejoy stacked the dishwasher. I fell asleep on the couch

14

ISN'T IT ROMANTIC?

Two months before our trip to Athens, Lovejoy reminded me that I had a CD coming due. It was one of mine that he had found out about when we prepared our income tax statement together for the first time.

"You have other CDs?" he had asked.

"This many," I said, holding the bank statements which declared the interest earned and which needed to be reported on our joint tax returns.

"This much money?" he asked, frowning as if disappointed to learn that we were four hundred and twenty-five thousand dollars richer than he had realized.

I don't know exactly why I told him about that money. I think I wanted to know if he would try to spend it. He did.

"We'll take care of this today," he decided, and together we drove to the bank, where he closed out a CD my late Aunt Felicia had left me—her favorite niece-- and deposited the twenty-five thousand dollars plus accrued interest in the joint bank account.

"We've got my retirement and my social security. We don't need this paltry interest on these CDs. Let's enjoy the money and not hoard it for later. We're neither of us spring chickens. There may not be a later."

I thought he would use the money to buy a car to replace his Buick, which was developing an unpleasant aroma now that the air conditioner didn't work. Frank's car smelled like wet clothes left in the washer for too long and then dried with the unpleasant stench of mildew to them. Yes, his car smelled disagreeably of mildew.

But I was wrong. Lovejoy didn't buy himself a new car. Frank wrote a fast check to the church to help build a home "for a woebegone family in the bad part of town."

Woebegone? Who uses that word and who is this man I married?

"I'm thankful we can help," he told me later after I asked him why almost ten thousand dollars was gone from our account. "I paid for our plane tickets to Athens and some incidentals."

The incidentals included another check for five hundred dollars to Marjeen and her baby. "Poor thing," Lovejoy said when he wrote the check. "Poor thing," he said loudly enough for me to hear him when he mailed it to her.

"Poor thing," I repeated after him, but I wasn't thinking about Marjeen.

******

We made love the night before the trip to Athens in my bedroom, and then he went to his room "...in order to get a good night's sleep," he explained.

Lovejoy

When I heard his door close and lock, I laid on my back and stared at the ceiling, the sheets warm and rumpled, my nightgown still on the floor beside me. "I wonder what Gigi really died from?" I whispered in the night to the memories of his two dead wives. Cardiac arrest and rectal cancer both make perfect sense.

The next day, squinting irritably because I had brought the subject up, he dismissively confirmed it. "Yes, Amanda died from a heart attack in her sleep."

"I thought it was the prayer closet," I interjected.

"Ah, bless her heart. Sweet Amanda collapsed in the prayer closet; but we moved her, you see. Then, she died. The Lord giveth...." Frank said, and then lost his train of thought. "Darla died from rectal something."

"Cancer?" I prompted.

"And the Lord taketh away. Of course. Blessed be the name of the Lord."

"When's the last time you had a physical?" I asked, for Lovejoy had not been to a doctor since we had married. Or if he had, he hadn't told me.

"Everything is up to date with me," Frank assured me, pressing his hand on the two passports and a sheaf of papers he said we would need when we got to Athens. Our bags were packed, the mail delivery put on hold, our money organized, and a check list made out and marked off. Lovejoy had a knack for traveling and a love for making lists

*****

The flight to Athens was longer and harder and hotter than I had imagined it would be, but Frank did not notice or tire. He

127

knew how to navigate the stop-over in the Atlanta airport. When we landed in Athens, he was not troubled by the moving sidewalks, the expanse of white walls, the intense sunlight pouring in through windows and skylights or the directions that contained words with odd combinations of letters. My husband's walking speed increased the minute he got off the plane. I tried to keep up with him and then contented myself by trailing behind, lugging the carry-on case that I had brought with me while he steered us to the baggage claim where an unshaven man in a thin white cotton shirt and baggy tan pants was holding a handwritten sign that said: Love+ joy.

As if they were old friends, Frank walked over and warmly greeted the man with the sign, turning to signal to me with a jerk of his head that I should join them.

The sign bearer wasn't the chauffer. He was the headmaster of a school for boys that was part of the group of ministries our church supported. Lovejoy had never met Sid before (that may or may not have been his real name), but Frank recognized Sid from his picture in the directory of missionaries that JD kept current. Missions Man is what Frank called JD, the chairman of the missions ministry, when he wasn't worried about how people thought he would sound.

Frank kept up a friendly chatter with Sid while signaling which bags were ours. Together, as if they had done it a hundred times before, my husband and his new best friend loaded the bags onto a rolling cart which materialized out of nowhere. Really. The cart wasn't there. Then the cart was there.

Lovejoy

When I asked Lovejoy, "Where did that cart come from?" he laughed in a way I had never heard him laugh before—free and robust--and said, "Honey, you are in Athens, the origin of civilization and art. The Acropolis. Mars Hill! Anything can happen here."

Sid's car was nearby. With an efficiency that would not have been possible if we had traveled with the other team members (Let's go on our own so we won't be held up by other members' travel problems, and they will have them. You can count on it!), we were soon safely inside Sid's car. He steered us into a stream of traffic headed exactly opposite of the direction where the buildings looked grander.

Lovejoy began to ask questions and receive answers to a slew of queries he had about where this or that was, including the original Olympics fields and the Acropolis. Frank and Sid laughed companionably when Sid explained we would be staying "near an outdoor café where they serve the best baklava and strongest coffee in all of Athens."

"Did you hear that, honey? Baklava!"

I didn't know what that was. Fatigue hit me, and I didn't want to know. I felt left out of this new friendship. I was tired and simultaneously jealous of my husband's zeal for travel and meeting people. Who was Sid anyway?

In the car that didn't have an air conditioner, we passed by some tall, fine hotels with air conditioning and drove for forty-five minutes before we reached a long flat building that would be our "campout headquarters."

Before I could say, "Will we have cable TV, air conditioning, and room service?" Lovejoy held up a hand and grinned. "Now you know this isn't a vacation we're on. We'll be camping right here, and you'll be just fine. People don't need as many creature comforts as they believe. It's good to experience that from time to time."

That's when a headache started at the base of my skull. By the time the car was unloaded, my eyes were throbbing, pain flooded me through my head and down my back, and I was certain if I didn't get inside a building with air conditioning where it would be cooler and hopefully darker, I would throw up.

A friendly woman who wasn't wearing any make-up and whose dark hair was twisted up in a ball on the back of her head, greeted us at the front door, dropping her head in a minimalist version of hello that had the effect of being a curtsy. We were honored guests. Even though my head hurt, I almost curtseyed in response, but she wasn't looking at me. Once our hostess lifted up her head again, she couldn't take her eyes off my husband. That happened pretty often. I looked at him too.

Frank was head-turning handsome and had a smile that could launch a thousand love affairs. "Maybe it had," I muttered to God, as I stepped closer to my husband and took his arm.

He didn't seem to know I was there—not really. He spoke, and nodded, and smiled, and I attempted to smile and nod too, but it was hard. I was very tired, very hot, and experiencing something I had never known before: I was terribly homesick.

I didn't call it that. I said, "I'm getting a migraine."

Lovejoy

Lovejoy turned and studied me. He placed his hand, which was surprisingly cool on my forehead. Then he said the most surprising thing: "You don't feel like you're running a fever."

I was hot enough that I should feel like I was feverish to someone else, I thought irritably. But what I said was, "You don't run a fever with a migraine. You throw up." As soon as I saw the bathroom, I hurried into it, and slammed the door behind me.

The hostess and my husband spoke quietly on the other side of the door while I waited for my body to object violently to being away from my home, but as soon as I took a wash cloth and put it on the back of my neck I settled down. Embarrassed not to have thrown up after such a dramatic exit, I opened the door again, let a small flicker of a smile cross my face, and said, "Sorry. I'll be all right," and that was all Lovejoy needed to hear.

"She might need to lie down for a while," Frank said to the hostess Alexa, who steered us to a tiny room with barely enough floor space for our suitcases. "She's never been out of the country before. I don't know how far she has even been from where she grew up."

"Atlanta," I whispered, but neither of them heard me.

Studying me with regret and a kind of fear that I was going to be a lot of trouble—those Americans! —Alexa pointed toward a bed that looked clean. It was almost a double bed but not quite a single, and we were both supposed to sleep there.

"Gigi, you need to stretch out for a while in the dark. Take a Tylenol and let yourself rest, while I get the lay of the land."

Frank was eager to leave the house and only paying punctilious attention to how I really was or what might happen to me next.

I nodded obligingly, wishing I felt better. But as soon as Frank and Alexa were gone, I sat down hard on the side of the bed and asked God to save me from this mission trip. There was a small mirror over what was supposed to be a dressing table, and I saw myself in it. My lipstick was long gone. Even my hair looked tired. It was stringy, oily. I should have gotten it cut! My shoulders slumped. My lower back seized up in a cramp that wouldn't release; and even though I was a Southern woman, I could not force a smile to my face. When I tried to fake it, my head truly began to hurt. Not wishing to really throw up, I leaned back on the bed and let my shoulders relax into the surprisingly soft mattress. I could hear street sounds of traffic and talking outside, and occasionally someone else arrived at the front door, was greeted and escorted down the hallway. I figured the other members of the mission team were arriving.

"One day down, six days to go," I told God. "I wonder what happens if you decide you want to go home early. I wonder how that works." I resolved to find out how to change a return ticket and get back to the airport whether anyone went with me or not.

"I bet they have taxis in Athens," I said to God, before blessedly, I fell asleep.

I do not know how long I slept, but it was later in the day when I came back to life. As if he had a hidden camera on me and was watching, Lovejoy materialized in the room looking fresh and rejuvenated by his travel and excursions into Athens. "The jet lag got you bad," he said without sympathy. It was just a statement.

He was smiling and the light film of sweat on him made him glisten in a kind of attractive healthy way. I hated him for that.

He took my hand, and asked, "Do you want to get up? You don't have to. You can stay right here, and I'll bring you something to eat in a couple of hours when they serve supper."

Before I could answer, he said, apologetically, "I don't think you'll like the food here. It's different from what you are used to, though they try to accommodate foreigners."

I had never been called a foreigner before. My eyes closed without my permission, and he took that as a no. Lovejoy left quietly, and I didn't hear him again until it was dark outside. He returned with a napkin on which was placed a kind of sandwich.

"Cheese and bread only," he promised, when he saw the fear of what kind of horse or goat meat might be inside two pieces of hard stale bread with little brown bugs baked on the top.

"No mayonnaise. I didn't want to risk food poisoning. Their refrigerator isn't working."

I struggled to sit up, rearranging the limp pillow behind me. Frank shifted the food to my lap, and I looked at it with fear and resignation.

He walked around the small square room as best he could while I played with the food. I could feel his growing impatience. At one point he opened the window blind, but a street light was shining directly in. I placed my hand dramatically over my eyes. Sighing, he closed it again.

"Are you going to try and get up? There are people you could meet. They are nice people."

I clutched the bedspread nervously. "You go back out and make my excuses. The flying took a toll on me. My head is throbbing."

He nodded. "We're just on the other side of the door and down the hallway," he promised. "Join us when you feel better." He placed his hand on mine. "You will feel better. You really will. Trust me."

I nodded wanly and motioned to him to go on. Back home he might have come over and kissed me good-bye, but not in Athens. Lovejoy turned and left me to die alone.

Once the door was closed again, I did wonder how he would get my body home if I died in Athens. And then I had the strangest thought: I wondered if Lovejoy would mourn if I died in Athens. And if I became sick—sick unto death-- how much trouble would he go to to help me? Would he recite easily the words: The Lord giveth and the Lord taketh away. First Darla. Then, Amanda. Now, Cindy. If I died, would he openly call himself a martyr? And how long would it be before other women were crawling over each other to try and sit beside a thrice-bereaved widower at church?

Laughter happened then on the other side of the door. I tried to count people by distinguishing voices, but all I could tell was that there were men and women. I didn't hear any children talking at all.

At one point I stood up and opened the blind and looked out at Athens. The night had fallen and the floodlight in the street blinded me.   I saw only shapes of buildings and movements of cars and heard the sounds of people who had a purpose and were headed to it.

My headache eased, and I went back to the bread and cheese on the dresser and pinched off a taste. The cheese was rich, sort of buttery, and kind of salty. The little dark flecks on top of the bread weren't gnats or any other kind of bug. They were some kind of spice. I didn't like the taste at first and then I did. The bread wasn't stale after all. It was just thick chewy slices of homemade bread. A cup of strong coffee was there too, which I had not seen before. It was stone cold now, but I sat on the edge of the bed and ate the bread and cheese and then I drank the cold coffee, and I felt better.

Even though Frank had been gone a long time, I told him as if he were right in the room with me listening, "I've decided not to die in Athens."

15

WITH A SONG IN MY HEART

B reakfast was early. Hard rolls, fruit, yogurt, and cold slices of more cheese and thin wafer-like meat that had bits of fat in it. They called it a Continental breakfast, but it wasn't like any Continental breakfast I had ever seen before.

Thankfully the coffee was very hot and strong. I drank three cups fast and ate a roll.

While I was sitting off by myself at the end of the table, the other travelers arrived with the energy of the purpose-driven, rustling up breakfast with zest and appetite. Lovejoy was among them. Already Frank was popular, the center of attention. He was fully engaged, but he kept his attention on me with a glance, sometimes out of curiosity and, other times, exasperation and impatience. The others nodded to me and swapped introductions (first names only and fast smiles all around!), but they were all in a hurry to get to work, and even the movement of acknowledging a slug like me was slowing them down. I made a private bet with myself that they had all read that Piper book! They knew their purpose—had a mission. That was it, I thought dully: 'I was on a mission trip, but I didn't have a purpose in Athens.'

"Is your head better?"

I nodded *yes* because I couldn't afford to say otherwise. The look in Frank's eyes was too disappointed in me already.

"You go on. I will be all right," I promised. I didn't sound confident. But it was what he needed to hear.

As I was thinking that, Frank placed his hand on my shoulder and said, "They are going to keep you inside out of the heat today to work with the refugee women making small leather goods. It won't be hard to do, and working with the rescued women will be easier and cooler than walking the streets passing out our batch of New Testaments and tracts. The color's not so very appealing. It is an unfortunate shade of pea green. But the New Testaments are compact and fit inside a pocket or a handshake," Lovejoy said, holding out his hand to me.

Automatically, a good girl trained to take any hand outstretched to me, I shook my husband's hand. As he let go, he pressed a small green New Testament into my palm. I was staring at it, surprised momentarily at the slick maneuver and wondered if that is how he gave out New Testaments to strangers, discreetly and carefully—like a spy passing along news from the mother country.

I think Lovejoy kissed my cheek good-bye, but I was so surprised by this sleight of hand maneuver that it was only after he and the others passed through the front door, calling out their farewells, that I felt the imprint of his lips on my face. Then, the hand that wasn't holding the New Testament went up and pressed the faint sensation of his imprinted kiss into my cheek.

When the door was open, the heat of the day poured in, and he walked out into it talking amiably with the others.

"I'll be here when you get back just like you wanted," I whispered, but he didn't hear me.

That first morning I lived in the shadows with the other women. They didn't speak English, and I couldn't speak whatever language they whispered among themselves. They didn't need to whisper. I could have heard everything they said and still understood nothing.

Days 2 and 3 passed with me sitting with these women and punching holes into key fobs, men's belts, and bookmarks. It was determined early on that I couldn't punch holes well enough to make the belts or key fobs or bookmarks. My holes didn't line up and the edges were ragged. The instrument—I think it was just an ice pick-- was hard to manage. I stabbed both my thumbs, both my index fingers, and almost landed the ice pick into my chest. I bled some. But if left alone, I could thread the tiny strips of green ribbon through the holes of the bookmarks and tie a knot. So that became my job.

By the afternoon of Day 3 so much silence had happened between us that when I quietly excused myself no one objected or probably even noticed. I was up to speed on tying the ribbons, and the women needed more time to make more of their souvenirs to sell on the streets. Bored and feeling out of place, I was tired of feeling imprisoned with these hard-working women who, I was told, had been rescued from a life of prostitution on the streets. Had we been able to speak a common language, I was supposed to tell them about salvation in Jesus, but there were no words between us that could be shared.

So, I decided to escape, grabbing my special travel purse Frank had ordered for me from some kind of online store. It had security zippers for pockets, and he had secured our emergency backup money in case he was pickpocketed. "It happens," he said, as he explained where the coins and folded money that "would work in Athens" were hidden.

I stood out in front of the house and snapped a picture with my cell phone so that I could get a taxi to bring me back if I had to do business with a taxi driver who couldn't speak my language.

I didn't think I would walk far enough to get lost or need a taxi; but truthfully, my body needed to move.

With no destination in mind, I ventured out into the neighborhood, counting houses, looking for a shop, or even a street vendor—some place where I could survey the souvenirs of Athens that tourists like me want, but all I saw was a street café where people were sitting outside and not looking miserable. There were tables shaded by white umbrellas and lots of trees encircling it. The cafe was a cheerful place with as many people sitting alone as had someone sitting with them. I chose a chair outside underneath a leafy tree in the far corner, where I would not have to make small talk with a nearby customer. I waited for a server to ask me a question I probably couldn't answer.

Nearby a couple was sipping some kind of cold drink with ice cream. When a young man finally hurried over and looked questioningly at me, I simply pointed to what they were drinking and held up one finger.

He nodded with understanding and disappeared again, returning swiftly.

He brought a beautiful thick white mug of ice cream with coffee poured over it and the hint of some kind of liqueur. I didn't know its name. Not having eaten much in four days, I slurped the coffee quickly and then spooned the ice cream. The server kept track of my progress and tilted his head.

I held up another finger, and he brought me another mug of coffee ice cream. A lovely warm feeling of well-being enveloped me. I settled back in my chair and enjoyed the sight of other people, some of whom spoke words I knew, while others talked in languages that sounded musical to me. I wanted to hum while they spoke, and I can't explain that—not really.

I was alone but with them, and I felt myself begin to grow at ease. Tension I had been unaware of softened, and the ice cream felt good on my stomach. I hadn't been very hungry since I had left America. My appetite resurfaced, and I wondered if I were brave enough to try and order something to eat.

People were looking at maps together, and once a tour guide came by and sent her group on without her while she sat across from me, studiously avoiding my presence. She was paid to answer tiresome questions from tourists, and she didn't want to do it for free for me while she was on her coffee break. If she hadn't looked so unapproachable, I would have asked her: "What do people order to eat as a snack here?" But she was living inside herself, so I didn't. I wondered how long her break would last and what time it was when suddenly I saw Lovejoy come into the circle of outdoor tables from the other side.

My husband wasn't alone. A beautiful, tall, slender woman with shoulder-length dark hair sat down across from him. With all the ease of a man who had been here the day before and probably the day before that, Frank motioned to a server and without conversation ordered for the two of them.

He was sitting back in his chair, his shoulders relaxed—his body comfortable in the environment. When he did speak, he leaned forward with the same friendly keen interest he had shown me during our first meal at the Country Club.

"So, this is what a mission trip is to you," I said, losing interest in the lump of ice cream melting in a puddle of coffee.

My server came over and tilted his head significantly, and I made the motion of writing out a bill. And then he spoke: "I'll bring it right away, madam."

He did, but I was in no hurry to leave. I sat in the shade of the fragrant tree, my body obscured by the tour guide, who checked her watch every two or three minutes and finally rose. When she stood, I thought Lovejoy might turn toward the movement and see me, but he didn't. He was paying close attention to his companion, and she was smiling warmly at him.

I knew the nature of her responsive smile. I had worn a version of her smile for a while after my first lunch with Lovejoy at the Country Club.

I wasn't smiling in that moment.

Lovejoy

It did occur to me to go over there with my bill and lay it down for Lovejoy to pay. After all he's the one who had made me come on this trip for which I had no purpose.

But I hadn't bathed well or done my hair properly since we had arrived, and I couldn't face a woman who looked as sophisticated as she did in my current state of dishevelment.

The server returned and helped me figure out the money. It was an awkward situation with me holding my purse open, the small green New Testament, Kleenex, a lip gloss all out on the table while the server helped me count the money from my black snap change purse. Embarrassed to be so confused and dependent on the kindness of strangers in a foreign country, I repacked the lipstick, the Kleenex, and my change purse but left behind the New Testament as an additional tip and because the sight of it with my husband across the way sitting next to another woman annoyed me.

Lovejoy never saw me, and I slipped away into the shadows in the direction the tour guide had gone. I saw her group ahead and thought about just slipping into it and disappearing forever into the crowd, but I knew that sooner or later I would have to return to the refugee house and sit with the rescued prostitutes.

I took my time, and when I finally reached our headquarters no one was waiting for me. I let myself in and went right to my room, where I pulled out the best cleanest clothes I had in the suitcase. I took a proper bath, did my hair sort of, put on my lipstick, and when Lovejoy finally returned at dinnertime, I was waiting for him, brightly.

His eyes lit up. "You're better."

"Yes. So much better," I assured him.

He looked pleased, and steered me to the communal dining room where roasted vegetables and some kind of sticky grain dish was the entrée. I ate enough to be friendly and sat quietly in the corner afterwards while the team compared notes about the day's work and the next day's agenda.

Lovejoy said I would be staying with the other indoor women again, and I nodded agreeably, my smile in place.

But the next day after he left with his bottle of water and banana, I grabbed my purse and went looking for a beauty parlor, where I had my hair washed and four inches of my expensively highlighted tresses cut off. The girl styled it better than I could do it myself in that poor excuse for a bathroom we had back at the house. Then, looking younger, feeling lighter and kind of smug for going out into the world alone, I strolled a couple of streets, keeping a sharp eye out for the mission team, but I never saw anybody I recognized. Ultimately, I landed in that same outdoor cafe, sitting at the same table as the day before. This time I ordered food. It turned out to be a platter of grilled vegetables seasoned with something I had never tasted before. It was the best meal I had had since arriving in Greece. For dessert, I drank only one cup of ice cream coffee and felt that warm glow from the liqueur I didn't recognize. Though I watched for him, my husband and the tall girl with pretty dark hair did not return.

I wondered where they were and what they were doing.

16

AIN'T MISBEHAVIN'

Frank didn't take a single day off from his labor in Athens, but the ladies who had come as companions to their husbands were offered a guided tour of Athens as their reward for coming alongside missionaries as cheerleaders. I finally decided that was my purpose. I was supposed to be a cheerleader. However, we were close to going home, and I nodded willingly to go on the Athens tour, though I had already made three trips out of the house alone that no one knew about. I felt pretty smug about that.

On the sixth day—the day before we were to leave-- it was hot, very hot. It was the hottest day of the week in Athens, and we were supposed to go on a tour of the city and see all the hot spots.

Lovejoy explained to me privately that the street team would meet up later with those of us who had been working indoors. "Who do you mean? Those of us?"

To my knowledge I had been the only English-speaking woman working inside.

"There are others. You haven't met them?"

I shook my head, no. He waved aside my confession of ignorance, and said, "We're having an early dinner together before we all head home tomorrow." He exhaled deeply and with great satisfaction. "Do you know why the Acropolis is important?" he asked under his breath. I kind of nodded. He flashed me a knowing smile and said, "There's a brochure in your welcome packet that tells you the background. You might feel better if you know why you are going to see something."

"Is it outdoors?" I asked, squinting. My traveling headache had abated, but the suggestion of prolonged exposure to the heat while trapped in an airless van with strangers caused my eyes to burn and water. My head began to ache.

"We have an early flight out tomorrow and a lot to do. Do you remember to leave the clothes you brought in the chest of drawers? Just act like you have forgotten them."

I nodded and wondered why we couldn't skip going to dinner or bed, and just go on over to the airport. It was very fancy and had colorful divans, luxurious bars, and an internet room. It would be cooler at the airport. I almost said that. I almost said, "Let's just catch a cab right now and head over to the airport," but Lovejoy was turning toward his co-workers, his co-missionaries, his new best friends.

He gave me a fast peck on the cheek and said, "We'll meet up with you at the Acropolis and have a high old time at a restaurant this evening where they serve shark."

"I don't want to eat shark," I replied.

"You can order whatever you want, but shark is their specialty. Imagine telling others back home that you ate shark. That's something, isn't it?" He waited for me to understand what kind of something it was, so I smiled grimly, and nodded. "I'll meet you at the Acropolis."

146

Lovejoy

He did his trick of leaning close and whispering in my ear "A you're adorable. B you're beautiful. C...." I never heard what C was. When I asked him one time what he whispered he smiled—his mouth two inches from mine—his blue grey eyes bewitchingly flirtatious. "It's the alphabet song. Perry Como used to sing it. Or maybe it wasn't Perry." He looked confused for a moment and then chortled softly to himself as if it was a joke. I didn't understand the joke.

I didn't know the song, but there were still moments past desire when I desired Lovejoy. In that moment I went a little weak in the knees, a response truly embarrassing. He seemed to know the effect he still had on me, and his eyes beamed with a kind of satisfaction that didn't set well with me. So, after that, when he whispered anything in my ear, I shifted my head gently in the other direction to avoid letting him know that he had that kind of power over me.

I went on the tour with more people I didn't know and without my husband in a small van that took us slowly, slowly through narrow streets crowded with tourists like us. It took hours of riding in the hot van to get anywhere at all. When someone called out the name of the destination and its historical significance, I couldn't see it because of the massive crowds of people, and I couldn't hear the description because of traffic and the din of yammering coming from the streets. I was sweating and nauseas. I was motion sick—or heat-sick— or homesick. I wanted my husband so I could yell at him. I wanted my husband so I could hide next to him. I wanted to cry. I wanted to go home.

When we finally reached the Acropolis, I couldn't get out of the van fast enough. They gave us some kind of skip-the-line ticket, and then Sid's wife—I guess Alexa was Sid's wife—took off in the direction of the steps which led up. She was wearing a light blue cotton dress and a sun hat with black sunglasses. Just sandals. No pedicure. No manicure. No makeup. She looked fresh as a daisy.

Though she must have seen the Acropolis often and close up every time a mission team came to stay and expected a tour of the hot spots after a week of being a laborer in the field, she led with the zest of someone who was a proud Greek. She was a hostess as eager for the trip to be finished successfully and good-byes of good will said as I was eager to leave and get home to my own bed. I think we all felt that way because no one was talking. We were close to the finish line, when all of a sudden, the theme song to "Chariots of Fire" began to play over a sound system. We all moved with great energy inspired by the music, our leader, and mostly motivated by the unspoken knowledge that once we had climbed this hill—the Acropolis—we had only one obstacle left before we could fly home. We had to eat a shark.

Sweat was pouring down my back as I moved. Concentrated on reaching the top, I discovered when I finally did that, I was there with a lot of other people but that none of them were members of my group. Sid's wife was nowhere to be seen. I pivoted slowly, massaging the base of my neck which was stiff with tension. I didn't see anyone I recognized.

I was not afraid at first, for I knew where I was supposed to find the van. It was just down below and a block or so over from the entrance, unless they had moved. Would they have moved the van? With my legs shaking from the strain of the climb I began to thread my way back down the steep steps only to discover that the movement of the crowd of tourists was like a riptide that had changed my direction. Going down I kept moving with the crowd and wound about in a way I had not planned to descend. Clutching my purse close to my midriff in case there were pickpockets in the crowd, I landed in a place at the bottom of the steps where I had not begun.

The van was nowhere in sight, and neither were any of the people from the van. That was the moment I began to worry. I had my purse, but my passport wasn't in it. Otherwise I would have comforted myself with the promise that I could hail a taxi, leave all the stuff in my room, and just go to the airport and wait there for Lovejoy to find me. Surely, he would come to the airport and find me. If he didn't, well….I was beginning to follow that thought when I realized that Frank had the plane tickets stored with our passports. I was stuck at the bottom of the Acropolis with just enough money to catch a taxi to get back to the lodge. I could do that.

A taxi would take me to the address in the picture of our building that I had on my telephone. In the meantime, I was lost in a foreign country, abandoned by the other members of the team, and surrounded by thousands of people, some of whom were tourists, others native to the country, and still others, refugees or potentially, I thought, terrorists.

"What am I doing here?" I breathed, and then I stopped moving. Just stopped. It felt to me that I had been in a kind of unfamiliar perpetual motion since the day Franklin Lovejoy had invited me to Sunday lunch and declared his intentions. Since then I had been moving, moving, moving, only I didn't know where I was going with him anymore than I knew where I was going without him at the base of the Acropolis. A refugee from the mission trip, I was lost, truly lost and alone in a way I had never been before. It was nothing like the perfect freeing aloneness of being outside naked under an evening sky in Amanda's swimming pool. It wasn't like growing up alone either, waiting on your life to begin. I was calculating the ways I had known aloneness, including during the days of my marriage to Lovejoy, when suddenly I heard my husband's voice calling out over the sea of people.

"Cindy!"

I pivoted slowly, listening.

"Cindy!"

I turned, and there several people away was Frank Lovejoy who was calling to me and working hard to get through the crowd; and just like in a movie, I pushed and pushed, moving my legs and using my hands to reach him. When I did, I collapsed into his arms, and my body shuddered in relief that I was as close to home as I could get in Athens. Lovejoy let me hold onto him as long as I needed, but when I was able to step back, he mopped his head with a white handkerchief but he couldn't make himself smile. He whispered in my ear, his voice laced with wonder and impatience: "How did you get so lost?"

Before I answered, he looked around, still blotting the sweat on his forehead with a kerchief. He wasn't wearing any of his colorful socks, bow ties, and matching handkerchiefs here. Everything Lovejoy wore in Athens was white, and that was the first time I noticed that about him. Six days of Lovejoy wearing mostly white, and I had not noticed before. He had not yet mentioned my haircut.

He looked down at me sadly and said in a mournful voice, "Everyone else went up and came down, but you got all twisted up, didn't you?"

"I have never had a very good sense of direction. I guess you just don't know that about me. One of the reasons I never went on mission trips was because I get lost. I get lost very easily."

Lovejoy nodded seriously, as if glad to understand something that was now patently and inconveniently obvious. "The rest of them are waiting by the van. Try to pull yourself together. We are going home tomorrow. You can hold yourself together for that long, can't you?"

I don't know what my response was—a nod, a swallow, a single movement toward him and the refuge of his strength, but when I was close enough to absorb any kind of help it didn't come. In that moment as we threaded our way back to the others, I was beside him but alone. It was a new kind of loneliness for me. Later, I would discover a name for it, but in that moment, I was only thirsty, tired, homesick, and despondently aware that on a mission trip I was a failure. I alone was a failure.

He took my arm firmly and led me to the van; and when we were inside, the others smiled forgivingly and companionably. I didn't like any of them. Out of the discipline of being a Southern woman, I smiled weakly back. I knew some of the names of the other trip members, but because I had stayed in the small house with the refugee ladies, we had not become traveling friends—friends with stories to share and tell, except this last one. I was the story, and they would be telling it.

"Frank's new wife got lost, and we had to find her."

That would be the story that was told about me.

"Frank's new wife slowed us down on our last day in Athens—the one where we were supposed to have some fun."

"We were sitting in a hot van while Frank looked for her. Poor Frank."

"He could have had any other woman at church. Why her?"

"He's such a good Christian man, and I remember hearing about her. Before Frank, she was kind of a trouble-maker—hard to get along with—you remember? Sometimes men like to marry trouble. Some men like the excitement of a high maintenance woman."

Frank was embarrassed by the problem I had caused, and I was embarrassed for him. Later when they served me a hard hunk of shark, I took small bites of it as penance and swallowed it with great difficulty but without complaint. Shark is oily and tough and hard to chew the way a pencil eraser is. It was the worst thing I'd ever put in my mouth—worse than shrimp and grits.

17

MY FOOLISH HEART

The plane trip home was long and uneventful. Whenever I needed to go to the Ladies' Frank mumbled the same thing, "Now don't get lost. Count the rows and come back to this one. We are eleven rows back."

I didn't mind him saying it the first time or the second time, but I did mind it the third time and the fourth. It was a very long flight. The fifth time he said something about my maybe needing to see a doctor about my condition when we got home. I said I needed to stretch my legs and my back hurt and the person on the other side of me kept wanting to put his head on my shoulder, and he mumbled, "Tell me about it."

Which is what I was doing. Frank wouldn't look at me, so once I was settled again, I said while staring ahead at the back of the seat in front of me: "I saw you with that brunette in Athens. You were sitting in the café leaning forward talking very intimately."

He heard my words, drawing up in his seat. I felt him turn toward me before he replied, "I was explaining the gospel to her. She accepted a tract we were handing out, and I took her for coffee in order to answer her questions."

"She looked very glamourous. Her hat had a turquoise scarf, and she was very beautiful."

"Beautiful women need salvation, too. It makes them more beautiful," he added cryptically.

"You always have a story like that," I said.

"And you're the hardest woman I have ever tried to love."

We finished the flight in mostly silence, each of us exhausted with the trip and each other.

When we got home, the house felt strange and smelled old. Frank dropped the mostly empty suitcases near the laundry room (we had brought back our underwear and night clothes), and we went to our respective showers. Nothing was said about managing our jetlag or eating supper. We each had a bowl of cereal with Almond Milk (one of Lovejoy's tricks for traveling. Regular milk goes sour, but Almond Milk stays fresh!), and he went to his bedroom and closed the door while I looked through the accumulated mail, throwing out the flyers, sorting the bills, and placing the three personal letters Lovejoy received on his desk. Then I listened to the answer machine. Pollsters. Telemarketers. Several hang-ups, which I found reassuring.

I sat in the living room for a while, growing drowsy and shaking myself awake. I didn't want to go to bed. To adjust to the change in time I needed to reprogram my sleeping. While I was telling myself that was the smart thing to do, I fell asleep and stayed in Lovejoy's recliner all night long, waking when I heard him shaving.

I stumbled groggily to the kitchen and switched on the coffeemaker and then went to comb my hair and splash my face. By the time he came out of his room the coffee was ready.

He walked by me to the kitchen and got a cup and then began to read his newspaper. "You won't believe what the governor has been up to while we have been gone," he said.

His voice was different. Much different than it had ever been. He was present and distant at the same time. He felt me looking at him and raised his head long enough to meet my eyes, then returned his attention to the newspaper, shaking his head at what he read. "Anything good come in the mail?" he asked absently, turning the pages.

"Bills. Expensive trash. A couple of love letters for you." My voice sounded bitter and caustic even to me. His head jerked up. "I placed them on your desk."

"Who are they from?" he asked.

"I assumed they are from your old admirers," I said, attempting to make a joke.

He looked up. "Don't ever read my mail," he said sternly. "This was my house before it became ours. I expect a certain amount of privacy."

I took a deep breath before answering, slowly. "I don't read your mail. And I don't want you to read mine anymore. When the bank sends me renewal notices, let me open them. I will tend to my CDs from now on."

He was in the middle of turning a newspaper page when I said that. He let it fall, his gaze growing opaque. He wasn't angry—just solemn.

"And I'll be deciding what to do with my money. We have been spending the principle, and I don't want to do that anymore. If something happens to you, I will need the income from my CDs to live. If they are gone, I won't have enough."

"Hoarding is unbecoming," he said. "What ever happened to love, honor, and obey till death us do part?"

I took a long time answering. My head was beginning to throb again. Jet lag pulled at me like a dark undertow. I was home, and the homesickness should have been cured. But it wasn't.

"Marjeen happened for one thing. And my house is gone. That's another. And since we've been married fifty thousand dollars in CDs is gone. Doesn't matter to me what you spent it on or how you gave it away. We can't keep spending my money. One day I could need the rest of my money. You're older than I am."

He muttered something under his breath, "Keep it up, and you'll be the death of me." But I'm not sure if he really said that. His head was down while he turned another page of the newspaper; and when he looked up, his signature smile was on his face. "Whatever you say, my dear. I've been trying to be helpful. You asked me to take care of the house. You asked me to take care of the bills. You asked me...." He didn't finish the last sentence.

"The trip to Greece was expensive. A check for the amount we spent given to them would have relieved those poor refugee women of having to make and sell a bunch of key fobs and leather bookmarks on hot Greek streets. Of course, then they wouldn't have the heartbreaking story to tell of making fobs and bookmarks, not to mention that refrigerator that didn't work. Bless their hearts."

He watched me with interest. "You are coming out from where you have been hiding for a long time." He let loose a sigh, and closed the newspaper altogether. "My work here may be done."

"What work is that?" I asked, going into the kitchen to pour myself a refill. I brought the pot back and held it over his cup. He nodded and I topped off his cup. His right arm encircled my hips, and in spite of the tension between us, he gripped me companionably. I stood there while he petted me amiably. "I'm going to trade the Buick for a new car with an air conditioner that works. I hope you don't think I'm being too extravagant."

We froze in that moment. The conversation could have gone one way or another. Neither of the directions it could take would help us find our balance. "Don't worry, my dear. I will buy my own car with our money. My money is our money, but I will spend it just that way for the car."

"Where is your money? Our money?" I asked. For we didn't discuss his finances. He was on all of my bank accounts, but I didn't even know how many he had or how much was in the accounts.

"There's always a little nest egg for expenses like this," he said, looking pleased with himself.

Two days later Lovejoy bought himself a smart little black Mercedes roadster. I don't know how much it cost, but his small sports car could only seat two people comfortably.

While he was buying the car, I went to a bank I didn't use and opened a new account in my name only. When the next CD came due, I would move the money over to that bank and link the account to accrue the interest. After I had to eat the shark, I decided I needed some privacy.

18

IT HAD TO BE YOU

"I will be gone most of the day," Frank said, placing his breakfast dishes in the sink. He had eaten a bowl of muesli with a half cup of vanilla Greek yogurt on it. Since we had come home from Athens, Frank couldn't get enough of that Greek yogurt.

"Where?" I asked. I know men don't like to be asked questions that hold them accountable; and I had resisted asking too often before, but the memory of that brunette in the Athens café made me think I wanted to know who my husband might be drinking coffee with in the United States.

Frank answered amiably, without defense.

"A retreat of sorts. Don't you ever want to be off by yourself and meditate and pray?"

"We just came back from a mission trip," I replied, stating the obvious.

"That was a working vacation. And it was two months ago. This is different. I will most likely be back tonight; but if something comes up, then I shall return, Lord willing, tomorrow."

Lovejoy often used that phrase "Lord willing" to build himself some wiggle room when explaining his itinerary. If something happened that changed his plans, the Lord willed it.

"Are you taking a bag?" I asked, drying my hands on a dish towel. A cold curiosity rose up in me.

"I don't think I'll need a change of clothes," he said, smiling blandly.

The look in his eyes dared me to ask him another question, so I didn't.

"And I hope you won't just sit here and wait for me to come home. You do that sometimes. We are all stewards of the time God gives us. Don't spend your life waiting for me, as much as I love that you love me." His voice almost mocked me when he said those words.

I felt cold inside.

"How did you spend your days before you married me?"

"Believe it or not, I had a life before you," I replied coldly.

"I know you were alive before you met me. But what did you do?" Frank asked easily. His voice changed with the question. When I turned to look at him, he was waiting for my answer—sincerely curious.

"Committees. Lunches with girlfriends. You know."

"Where are your girlfriends now?" he asked. "No one calls you much. No one comes over. What happened to your friends?"

As it turned out, I had mostly belonged to groups of women who identified themselves as single or divorced. When I married Lovejoy, I was ejected from the groups, as if by marrying him, I had somehow betrayed the unwritten laws of our loosely organized associations by singles for singles and that included widows.

I had not missed the girls really until that moment. When I began to compare the intensity of my life now with the lack of intensity previously shared with gal pals, I was stopped in my movements, looking at Lovejoy who was moving around the kitchen tidying the dish towel and rinsing out the coffeemaker. He was growing increasingly tidy, and it annoyed me.

"What do your friends do now?" he asked, turning to face me.

"I don't know," I replied, honestly.

"What did you do before—before we married—what did you do?"

"Played golf. Went to jazz clubs. Yoga class. Hiked in the Smoky Mountains. House sat for married friends. Pet sat for married friends. Babysat for married friends. And in-between, we waited and dated. Dated. Waited."

"Women do those sorts of things. Men date, but they don't wait. Not like women do."

"What are you getting at?" I asked.

"Just shooting the breeze," he replied, breezily.

No, he wasn't. His current of conversation contained a kind of jabbing small talk that had begun when I told him that I was going to take care of my own CDs. He didn't know about my new bank account.

"Do you want me to do anything for you before I leave?"

I leaned against the sink, the water drops on the counter seeping into the back of my shirt. "Like what?" I asked.

"Do you need any money?"

I shook my head. It was the first time he had asked that question.

He came to me and stood close, asking his next question in a tone of quiet intimacy that he didn't use very often anymore. "What would you ask for if you could have anything you want? Anything at all?"

'A happily ever after ending,' I thought, without hesitation. But I was becoming a realist and also someone who kept what she really thought to herself. After a long pause, I looked up at him and told him a version of the truth: "I don't know. It has never occurred to me that I could have exactly what I want."

He leaned into me, nuzzled my neck—let me know his warm presence which had once upon a time stirred me so easily. My body felt wooden—unmoved, and he understood. He stepped back and lightly gripped my shoulders. He eyed me squarely and asked, "Can I trust you to be here when I get back?"

I nodded docilely, and he leaned over and kissed me lightly on the lips.

Here's the strange part. My eyes stayed closed long after the kiss had ended; and when I opened them, he was staring at me curiously. Then, his attention shifted, he grabbed his straw hat with the black band that he wore at The Grand Hotel in Point Clear, and said, "I'm gone." His hand fished out the keys to his Mercedes, and he left by the front door, where he stood taking in the sight of the clear sky, the fresh breeze, a day which for him was filled with possibilities. "I'll be home when I get home," he said, closing the door after him.

He left me like that.   It was a remarkable moment for me, because it was the first time he had left me when I didn't feel the loss of him. I felt relieved and almost glad. That's when I answered the question he had asked: "I wanted you to be who I thought you were."

As I watched him back out of the drive way in his new black sportscar, I said loudly, "But you're not."

19

THE GLORY OF LOVE

The second time I followed my husband was to the Gulf of Mexico. I didn't know who he was meeting, but I didn't believe that stuff about a spiritual retreat. I didn't know what I was going to do if I saw another woman. I just knew that I needed to find out—to know with certainty what my husband was up to, and so I followed him.

It's about a three-hour drive to Point Clear, but it felt longer since I was hanging back, following Lovejoy. Fifty miles down the road, I recognized the familiar rest stop where he would pull in. When he did, I hung back over by the trucks until I saw him come out again. Keeping a distance, I fell in behind him. I was pretty sure I knew where he was going because he had snagged his straw hat with the black band. That is the hat he always wears in Point Clear when he wants to look like he belongs to a kind of low-key but posh resort city by the gulf. It's the hat he wears when we stroll the promenade at sunset at the rear of the Grand Hotel. It is the place where we went on our honeymoon. Point Clear is the romantic setting where, I know, Frank Lovejoy feels most at home as his most romantic self.

The memories of our honeymoon were present in me as we drove, and there was a moment when I thought he saw me in his rear-view mirror. I lifted my foot from the accelerator and fell back though I was pretty sure I was far enough back to be mostly a colored blur in his rear-view mirror. It's a good thing I slowed down though because a patrolman was banked on the left side of the road holding one of those radar guns. It doesn't seem fair to me that policemen lie in wait to catch the citizens they are supposed to protect and serve and give them a speeding ticket, but it happens all the time. Neither Lovejoy nor I got pulled over for speeding, but it was his foot hitting the brakes that illuminated his tail lights and caused me to hit the brakes on my car that saved us. We both sailed scott-free past the poor schnook who did get pulled over.

At the exit to Bay Minette, Lovejoy made the right-hand turn, but I did not. I couldn't really. The road he turned onto was two-lane and slow. There would be no traffic to hide behind—no cars to leave in between us camouflaging me and keeping him from knowing that he had a suspicious wife who was following him to a hotel he knew very well. But by then I was sure I knew where he was going. I just didn't know who he was going to meet. I knew one more thing: I wasn't just following him for my own curiosity's sake. Somewhere between going to Athens and coming home and getting over jet lag, I had decided that my future with Lovejoy was going to be short-lived. He was a wonderful lover, and I would miss his lovemaking. But it turned out that when I confronted that question about my heart's desire, I actually wanted more than I was willing to settle for with him. I wanted the love that I thought Lovejoy was offering me when he had proposed and when I had accepted.

I was ready to confront the effects of the truth. I was married to a man who had a way with the ladies. I just didn't know which lady had helped buy him that Mercedes.

*****

I parked my car across the street from the Grand Hotel and walked through the gate toward the conference center and down the sidewalk and toward the valet station where a generous tip should tell me where his car was parked so that I could avoid it.

Only the valet handling car parking duties that day had an answer I didn't expect: "There hasn't been a well-heeled dude in a black Mercedes coupe all morning. We haven't seen one of those since...." He began and stopped himself when one of his brother valets shook his head solemnly. He faced me and said plainly, a member of the fraternity of good old boys who never tell on other good old boys and who work at a hotel where privacy is respected and precious information is studiously kept from curious wives or ex-wives or jealous lovers: "We haven't had a guest here recently who fits that description."

I almost laughed out loud. "No distinguished well-to-do man in a snazzy hat with an air of belonging?" I said.

They shook their heads no, which was a lie. Distinguished, well-heeled men who wear snazzy hats are the only kinds of men who can afford The Grand in Point Clear.

I nodded that I understood the code of silence was in effect. "Men will be men, and boys will be boys," I muttered, and waving au revoir as if I didn't care, I went looking for some lunch.

I was starving and passed through the main lobby to freshen up and then on to Bucky's, a small bar situated at the back of the hotel with a full view of the gulf, the boardwalk, and the pier. You pay for the view. A hamburger costs fifteen dollars at Bucky's, and it is worth it. Or at least it was when I had one for the first night of my honeymoon. Lovejoy had been amused by my appetite that evening. I had sipped a large glass of red wine, and he had ordered a fancy martini with extra olives, and "Make it dirty," he said with a wink.

I ordered a second glass of the house red for that wink. Then while I ate my charbroiled hamburger, Frank sat contentedly back in his chair, his thoughts going elsewhere while he toyed with a Caesar salad and a small order of crab claws. He selected a crab claw thoughtfully, slowly—one petite crab claw at a time, dipping them in the red cocktail sauce and discarding the shells with finesse. He treated the salad as if it were made up of garnishes. He ate leaf by leaf, shoving aside the croutons until he made a little hill of them on the corner of his salad plate. "There's something rather unseemly about a crouton, as if it was supposed to become something real and was thwarted in its ambitions. And they are often stale it seems to me, and lacking in flavor. I've never found croutons worth my attention. Stale crumbs of bread! Life is meant to be more of a banquet than a crouton represents."

Lovejoy

I thought Lovejoy was brilliant and charming the first time I heard that. Later, crouton after crouton, explanation after explanation, I didn't think the oft-repeated observation was that brilliant or charming. Usually while he explained at length to a new listener the reason for the pile of croutons on his plate, I just reached over, scooped up his scorned croutons and ate them one by one like popcorn.

That night when our honeymoon meal was finished, my plate was empty, and I was full. He had eaten enough of his to say he had eaten, but when the server came to take his plate, she picked up mine without question and then looked at his and said, "Was everything okay with your food, sir?"

He offered the server one of his signature smiles. While I didn't have a name for it that night, I learned over time that Lovejoy has a forgiving smile that could cause people to believe they had done something wrong for which they needed to be forgiven. In his defense he used his forgiving smile generously. He had an inventory of other smiles, too. His smiles told his moods: delighted, amused, enraptured by you and you and you. Strange how someone's inventory of smiles can cause you to take an inventory of yourself. I was just wondering what my smiles looked like to others when my cell phone buzzed. Two messages came through from earlier times. The signal must have been slowed down. Both messages were from Lovejoy.

The first read: Missing you already. Enjoy your day. Do something nice for yourself.

The second message said: I may be delayed. Don't wait supper.

He had already told me that once before. I figured a guilty conscience makes you repeat yourself.

I placed my order for a honeymoon hamburger and wondered if I dared to take a walk afterwards on the pier before heading home. I felt free and relieved. It's one thing to suspect your husband is unfaithful; it's quite another to postpone having to find out for sure.

The hamburger arrived hot and steaming with dinner fries on the side. It also came with individual size bottles of ketchup and mustard. They amused me. 'When emptied and washed out, the miniature bottles would make cute little salt and pepper shakers,' I thought, only you would have to poke holes in the lids. I winced when I recalled how poorly I had been able to punch holes in the leather goods. The idea took me back to Athens and the refugee women and the coffee ice cream and the sight of my husband with that model with the slender legs and the white dress and the straw sun hat with a flowing turquoise scarf that she kept pushing out of her way but without irritation. Every time the breeze caught her scarf, she rearranged it to drape across her shoulder and onto her breast, and every time Lovejoy had smiled at her. Smiled. 'What kind of smile is that?' I wondered, remembering.

"That's a lot of food for one person," the waitress said, without smiling. Her name tag said Denise. And even though I read names on tags all the time, I routinely think that's not really their name. That's the name they use so that people can speak to them. Surely, they keep their real names private.

Denise topped off my glass of water, and I said, "I'd like some iced tea after all."

Lovejoy

As often happened whenever I was near the gulf, the tension in my shoulders began to dissolve, and parts of me that stayed braced for living relented of their control. Every time someone opened the door to the patio the gulf breeze came in, and I began to think that maybe nothing was wrong after all and that I could simply relax and let go. Maybe I could live happily ever after anyway. My breathing slowed, and I began to imagine what I would really like to do.

"Here's your bill, whenever you're ready," Denise said, laying it face down and tapping it twice, some private movement of hers meant to make sure I saw it and would pay it.

I nodded and wondered if the spa could give me a facial and a massage and a pedicure. I longed to sit in the hotel spa Quiet Room where it is dark, cool, and private with my legs stretched out on the wooden chaise while I sipped a glass of lemon water. Why couldn't I do that? Lovejoy was not going to be home. We could both be on our respective retreats.

Just as I was considering seriously going into no man's land—the spa-- a third message arrived.

"Won't be home tonight. Lock your doors and wait for me. See you tomorrow."

I chewed my hamburger slowly, barely aware of the waitress who was keeping an eye on me. When I began to reach around on the floor for where I had parked my purse, she said, "You can charge it to your room. What's the number?"

"I'm not a guest of the hotel today," I told her, extracting my wallet. "I'm just a tourist traveling down memory lane," I explained, as I placed a twenty and a five inside the leather wallet that contained the bill. "No change," I said with a smile. "And is your name really Denise, or do you ladies choose a name to use while you are working here?"

Denise took the leather wallet with the money, and said, "It's my name." And then something outside the window caught her eye, and she remarked, "Well, look there. He's back again." I followed her gaze.

Lovejoy walked by and stopped by the wooden boardwalk swing where we had rocked gently watching the sunset three nights in a row on our honeymoon. He didn't sit down today. Instead he kept strolling toward the pier at the end of the hotel's boardwalk. When he reached it, he turned onto the pier that stretched out into the gulf, moving sanguinely along in his straw hat and his seersucker suit, his arms swinging gently and composed.

"Do you know him?" I asked, rising. My legs were stiff, my knees awkward. Driving had taken a toll. I needed that massage. That facial. That pedicure. That Quiet Room where women didn't need to be afraid that anyone will hurt them or rob them or lie to them or cheat on them or arrange a pre-marital counseling session with the preacher in order to get a pre-nup signed to protect his holdings.

"Yes. He used to come three or four times a year. He hasn't lately; but when he does, he sits out there on the end of the pier for a long time. When it gets later in the afternoon he comes inside and has a martini. He is not in a hurry. He takes his time with his cocktail, and then orders crab claws and a salad he just fiddles with. If he doesn't want to leave, he orders another martini. He doesn't like to talk, but a girl who used to work here—Brianna's gone now—said that she asked him one time if it was some kind of anniversary. The way he sat with an empty chair across from him—the way his thoughts were so present, so sad. Brianna said he looked so soulful and lost and lonely-- like he was missing somebody. He didn't answer her right away; but when he did, she said he had the sweetest smile and eyes the color of...."

"The ocean," I said before she could tell me.

That was a mistake. Denise almost didn't tell me the rest of it. Almost didn't finish the story.

"What other color could they be for such a romantic figure? Look at him. Very Gatsby."

"Who?" she asked, shrugging. She picked up my plate with her free hand, signaling to me again that it was time to move on.

"Who was he missing?" I asked.

"'All the women I have ever loved,' he told her. And then, you don't expect a man like that to brag, but she said that he smiled broadly—really big—and laughed when he added, 'And there have been a lot of women. A lot of women.' My friend thought he was hitting on her right then. You know how a man can sneak up on you with charm when he knows he's got a way about him that women like, and that man out there on that pier has got a way about him. Brianna said that she knew what he was thinking, and she said that even though she knew what he was thinking—and he was thinking mighty highly of himself—that she had been kind of interested in him."

Lovejoy turned, facing the other direction. He was wearing his straw hat with the black band. He had a nice gait, a mysterious purposeful bearing. The sun fell on him kindly. Others on the pier turned to look at him as he strolled by.

"Brianne said that if she hadn't had to work, she might have said yes. She said, 'I was that curious about whether he was the man he thought himself to be.'"

"The man he thinks himself to be," I repeated.

"But he's gotten older since I've been working here for three years. I brought him a martini once. This was a couple years back, and I brought him a salad and something else, I don't remember what. He stays a while, looking at the piano over there. Once I thought he wanted to play it, but when I told him it would be all right, he said he didn't play the piano. 'I used to sing some,' he said, and telling me that made him sad. He stares out at the water while he eats and his face grows still and sad, and I just thought, 'Whoever she is, better her than me. Better her than me. There's one born ever' minute. Some women fall for the sorrowful romantic type, but not me. I don't fall for that type."

Denise left then, if that's her name. She left me with my thoughts and no change and only one safe way to exit quickly before Lovejoy decided to come in and order that martini and move from one pose to another: a romantic figure that others watched and talked about.

'He would like that,' I thought. I walked right past the spa on my way to my car, all thoughts of the Quiet Room with its serene shadows and the peace of isolation and protection forgotten, left behind the steam bath where you can sit wrapped in thick towels among strangers in a room where the intimacy of dark and steam and sometimes whispered confessions is the reward for paying the spa fee.

*****

Three hours later I eased up into Amanda's driveway as the sun was just falling behind the gulf water. Lovejoy was probably watching the sunset from inside Bucky's, sipping his martini now, nibbling on crab claws and toying with a piece of lettuce after he had scraped off the croutons. *What did he do afterwards? Did he smile at the ladies? Did someone meet him? Did he take one last stroll down the promenade landing where his car was discreetly parked?* I didn't know where. I never saw it.

What kind of homage is it when you sip a martini and toast all the women you have ever loved? And there have been a lot!

"I wonder how many times he has done that," I said before heading to the shower. That walk to the shower was perfectly composed. I remember how my feet hit the carpet, landing solidly with each step. I peeled off my traveling clothes.

Once the spray of hot water was coursing down upon me, I began to scream, the cries leaving my body in anguish so deep I didn't recognize the sound of myself.

My shoulders shook with heaving and the cries abated, finally, when I turned off the water and stuffed a towel against my face. I slumped to the floor of the shower and let the water drain from my body, my hair drying on its own while I sat crumpled and naked.

My body ached with driving and suspicion.

My joints hurt from holding myself together.

I knew I needed a plan, but I did not know how to make a plan. There was no one to talk to—no one at all. "In my whole life I've never really had a plan," I said aloud, with wonder. It might have been a prayer. I'm not sure.

Finally, because I was cramped and uncomfortable, I stood up and opened the glass door of the shower stall and stared at myself in the mirror naked. There was no beauty or mystery in my appearance. I was a middle-aged woman with stringy wet hair and only a couple of kinds of smiles that have very little effect on anyone else. I knew who I was, and I couldn't compete with brunette models in Athens with long legs and hats with scarves. I couldn't compete with anyone, and if I could, I didn't have the energy. As I toweled off, I had the most amazing idea: I wasn't sure I wanted to win if I could compete. I was just facing that idea when I heard the front door open.

"Gigi, I'm home!" Frank called out.

I looked at my face to see how much it told. Nothing.

"Great. I'm in the shower. Be out in a minute."

I wrapped a towel around myself and stepped out. Lovejoy was standing in the doorway smiling at me.

"When did you start wearing a towel to come out into your own bedroom?"

He eyed me curiously.

"I thought you were going to be gone all night," I said, ignoring his question.

Lovejoy

He moved at the same pace that he walked the boardwalk and the pier toward me, grasping my shoulders and peering deeply into my eyes. I could see the ocean in his eyes, and he looked pleased with himself. I wondered if he had met Denise.

"Have you eaten?" he asked, though it was past eight and he knew that we now kept Early Bird dinner hours. "What have you been doing? You haven't just been waiting for me, have you?"

"I ate," I said. "Why'd you come home early?"

"Just couldn't stay away from you another minute is all."

He looked around the room. And for a second, I thought he was going to check the shower or under the bed to see if I had a lover stashed there. *Really? Really? Had he come home early expecting to find me with someone else?*

He kissed me good-night and headed to his room. "It's been a long day. If you're all right, I'm going on to bed."

I walked over to my bedroom door and closed it, too. Then, leaning against the door listening for him, my right hand found the lock and twisted it. It clicked. I wondered if he heard it.

Going to my bed, I dropped to the floor beside it onto my knees for the first time in a long time and prayed, "What have I gotten myself into?

20

I'VE GOT IT BAD
AND THAT AIN'T GOOD

Lovejoy steered Marjeen in his gentlemanly fashion out to the chairs by the pool, which we now no longer discussed. For all kinds of reasons, I resented Lovejoy sitting by Amanda's pool speaking with Marjeen who couldn't stand me.

Marjeen held her small boy-- Lovejoy's responsibility-- against her chest. I watched them settle down, their chairs turned at angles where they could talk but not exactly face one another.

What does one do when another woman comes over with a toddler and wants to see your husband alone?

Do you offer iced tea?

Lemonade?

I thought about going out there as naked as the day I was born and swimming laps while they tried to talk. But I didn't. I watched covertly from inside instead.

Marjeen passed the boy over to Lovejoy to hold. He took the baby boy easily, and no man did that without having held other babies, other children. *What other babies had he held*?

A sudden start of fear and curiosity produced another question: *How many other babies was he responsible for? Lovejoy received lots of letters.*

They visited outside for about an hour, and then Lovejoy came inside and walked past me to his office, where he extracted the household checkbook and wrote a check to Marjeen that had both our names on it. He signed his name, holding it up to blow on the ink in a move that had not been necessary since ball point pens had been invented. 'The movement dated him,' I thought, as his pursed lips made the motion of blowing hot air on his name.

I was beginning to have a lot of thoughts like that.

'How much?' I wondered, but I couldn't ask. We had already had the Marjeen and baby discussion. When I pressed my husband about it, he patted my face for the first time in a conciliatory gesture he had not used before and said, "Wild oats, my dear. We all sow them, and we all pay the consequences. I am not exempt. Neither are you."

As I was staring out the window while he handed Marjeen a check, I thought: "I'm paying for your wild oats."

Marjeen didn't come back through the house. Instead, Lovejoy escorted her through the side gate and around to her car, which was parked behind mine. He opened the door for her, and she settled the child into the car seat in the back, and then he walked Marjeen to the driver's side. I couldn't see very well—couldn't see at all really.

Did he know that?

I saw him lean forward and then pull back. I know that motion. He kissed Marjeen good-bye.

Lovejoy

I know he kissed Marjeen good-bye, but what kind of kiss was it? Did I really believe that story he told me about Marjeen being his daughter by a woman who turned out to be a wild oat? A wild oat! Did I believe that? Would Alfred Hitchcock? I wondered.

Marjeen backed out of the driveway and drove away. Only then did Lovejoy go back through the gate and return to the chair by the pool facing the one vacated by Marjeen.

I gave him two minutes and then called out, "Are you thirsty?"

He didn't hear me.

I poured him a glass of ice water and took it to him, placing it on the small table between the two chairs. He looked up, surprised by my presence, and made himself smile.

"That was hard," he said.

I was supposed to feel sorry for him. I didn't, but I nodded sympathetically anyway.

My hands rested on the back of Marjeen's chair. "Do you want to be alone?"

He struggled to answer. "Of course, not," he said finally.

I knew he wanted to be alone, but I sat down anyway.

"I fear Marjeen will have a rough time ahead. She's not very bright."

I didn't want to discuss Marjeen's IQ or lack of it. So, I asked, "Hungry?"

"I guess it is time to eat," he said tiredly, rising. He reached out and touched the back of my chair as if I needed help from him to rise. The move annoyed me, reminding me of that first time Frank had taken me to lunch, helping me in and out of cars and chairs before we ended up in front of that decrepit house where he had kissed me. I had the strangest thought in that moment as I stood and placed my hand on his wrist in thanks: 'Was Lovejoy a good kisser or had it been so long since anyone had kissed me that I credited him with a skill that was only part of being a man who knew where to place his mouth?'

As if reading my mind, he leaned over and placed his lips on mine. There was warmth and affection in the kiss but no curiosity. Was desire a form of curiosity really, and was he bored with me?

I kissed him back and thought again about finding a lawyer. And then I thought: 'Maybe Marjeen needs one too.'

21

THE WAY YOU LOOK TONIGHT

t was early so I poured us each a large glass of wine while some fish cakes baked in the oven and green English peas simmered on the stove. Neither of us was excited about the menu, but eventually you don't really care what you eat for supper. That's a sad truth. After Marjeen's visit, Lovejoy drank his wine quickly and poured another glass. The alcohol hit him on an empty stomach, and he began to talk about his past freely in a way he hadn't before.

"I got hired on the cruise ship where part of my duties was dancing with the single ladies. I was good at it.

"Singing in a night club is one kind of entertainment, but working a cruise ship is another. I preferred the latter, but I only did it for two years. Maybe that's why I think I preferred it."

"If you liked it why didn't you do it longer?" I asked carefully.

In the past he had not liked for me to ask him questions about his work. He would simply say, "History. It's all history now." And he would wave his hand in the air as if erasing some fact that I could have seen if I had looked harder.

Tonight, it was all present in him—not history at all, and he wanted to talk.

"As strange as it sounds, I got fired. 'Let go' was what they said. That's a terrible thing to say to anyone, isn't it? I'm letting you go. These days they call it being made redundant."

"Why?" I asked simply. I had never been on a cruise ship. The idea of a cruise ship made me claustrophobic. I had heard the rooms on a ship were small (maybe smaller than the one we had in Athens!), the hallways that led from the front to the back of the ship were narrow, and they assigned you to sit at a dinner table with a bunch of people you didn't know and may not come to like or enjoy. Who wants to eat dinner like that every night and pay for it too?

"I guess I was really too old when they hired me, and the night life took its toll quickly on the ship. At night I sang and danced with the ladies. In the mornings, I put on a suit and waited tables in the dining room. The ladies who danced with me at night didn't recognize me in the morning."

I wanted to ask him if he slept with them, but I was afraid of learning the answer.

"I loved the music though. There was a boy who played the piano for me. He was older than he looked—a pretty thing. I sang. He played. We were quite a duo. I can tell you that. We didn't have much time to practice. They liked us to take requests anyway, and I worked the audience, rounding up requests. That part unnerved me at first until I realized that the same songs get requested over and over again. If you can sing "My Funny Valentine" "All of Me," "The Way You Look

Tonight," and any other song Frank Sinatra made famous, you can make it on a cruise ship, if not New York."

"Until they let you go," I reminded him.

"Until they let me go," he agreed, tiredly. I tipped the bottle of wine toward his glass, and he nodded yes.

"That's a terrible thing to say to someone. I'm letting you go. Don't you think that's a terrible thing to say?" he asked.

I was startled. *Did he know he was repeating himself?*

"Did you keep company with the ladies on the ship?" I asked, delicately.

He nodded, his gaze as far away as the horizon on the Gulf of Mexico. "And there were a lot of ladies. I've always had a way with the ladies, but then I shouldn't have to tell you that."

"You don't have to tell me," I assured him, drawing back. My shoulders ached with trying to hold them back, and I felt very tired.

"Very few women can resist the line "Keep that breathless charm. Won't you please arrange it because I love you...." His voice shifted and he sang that last part, sadly, as if he were mourning a time gone by. His voice was uncertain, scratchy. I couldn't imagine him ever making a living singing with that voice.

"Did you love them?"

"Every single one of them," he declared emphatically. "They don't believe you can love every single one of them, but I did. Every time! I've always loved every woman who loved me."

It was five o'clock in the afternoon by the time we reached this point in the conversation. Lovejoy checked his watch, and his features readied. A light was forced into his eyes. I had never witnessed him turning on that light before. He turned on his breathless charm by will and with practiced perseverance. The light of interest and romance showed up in his eyes and in a disarmingly sincere, though I saw in that moment, practiced smile. 'He has made an appointment in his mind with me for love,' I thought. He has made an appointment in his mind with me for love, and I felt sorry for him. Protective, too. I wanted to relieve him of the responsibility of me.

I reached out and took his hand and placed it on my chest right in the center.

He looked into my eyes and said, "Gigi, A you're adorable. B you're so beautiful. C...." his voice trailed off.

"I bet you sing that to all your girls," I theorized.

He thought I was flirting with him, and it pleased him.

But I wasn't. I was telling him the truth. I bet he sang that alphabet song to all the girls he's loved before.

"How would you feel about going out for an Early Bird supper now? You didn't have lunch. And you know you don't want those fish cakes. We could throw them in the trash."

He exhaled—relieved that he could let go of his responsibility to prove to me how adorable I was and how good he was with the ladies. I suggested the steak house nearby where it was 2 for 1 sirloin night, with baked potato and broccoli included.

"Let's go," he said, with forced zest. He looked tired, and I wondered how many times he had manufactured an enthusiasm for going out with a woman in order to eat dinner and avoid lovemaking. He was letting me go. I was letting him go. We didn't call it that. We called it going to an Early Bird dinner.

I grabbed my purse, and as he took my elbow and steered me to the passenger side of my car, I asked him, "Did the women tip you on the ship?

"Yes," he said simply. "I earned more tips than any other man on the ship."

"Why don't I drive tonight and you look at the stars?" I suggested. He had drunk too much.

He didn't hesitate. Glad to forfeit the responsibility of driving us, Frank settled into the passenger seat and mused aloud, "I miss getting tips. There was something gratifying about knowing how much you were appreciated."

He waited for me to say something that would make him more comfortable. I told him a strange truth that was growing stronger and stranger every day. "I love you, Frank," I said simply.

But love wasn't what I thought it was, and love inside a marriage changes. We were growing older together slowly, but I could barely keep up with the pace of love changing quickly in him and, mysteriously, in me.

22

DAYS OF WINE AND ROSES

Lovejoy was awake before I rose the next day. I found him sitting at the kitchen table working the crossword puzzle and nursing a large mug of coffee.

"You okay?" he asked, barely looking up.

"Sure," I said, kissing the top of his head as I headed to the coffeepot. Looking down I saw he was wearing his bedroom slippers. He couldn't face me.

"You need anything while I'm up?" I asked.

I moved to stand beside him, and his arm encircled my waist, like always. His arm felt bony against my flesh. A trembling occurred, and he pressed harder against me to stop it. I let him linger there until he could trust himself to let go.

Eventually, the smell of his coffee drove me to go get my own, and he reluctantly released me, slapping my fanny as I walked away. I was supposed to chuckle, so I did.

"What's your day like?" he asked, when I sat down across from him. His spine stiffened, and I saw him ready himself to listen to me with interest.

"What do you want it to be like?" I asked brightly.

"I thought we might go for a drive," he said, looking up. His eyes were different. Anxious. Vulnerable. He couldn't look at me for long. I wanted to reach over and pat his hand and tell him it was all right, but he couldn't have borne that. So, I smiled instead.

"I don't usually drink that much," he explained unnecessarily. He usually kept me from drinking a third glass of wine. We had never had a fourth glass of wine together before. There were two empty wine bottles in the kitchen trash can.

"Who cares? You were home. You can let go at home."

"I talked a lot," he said, searching my gaze for clues about what I had heard and remembered.

"You said you used to sing. I have heard you sing harmonies in hymns at church, but at home I haven't heard you do much more than hum."

"I regret to say that I think my singing days are behind me," he said. "Like my dancing days," he added. "You know I love you, don't you?"

"Yes," I said. "I know you love me."

You always love the ladies who love you.

Satisfied, he turned his attention to the puzzle in front of him, and his hand clasped the handle of the coffee mug. His fingers trembled again.

"I could take you out on the boat," he offered, finally. His back straightened and his head went back with determination.

"That isn't necessary," I said, primly.

"You like to go on the boat," he stated.

"I'm fifty years old. I can be happy not going on the boat," I promised.

He wasn't sure what I meant. And then a faint smile tugged at the corners of his mouth. "I remember the day we met with the preacher for counseling. You told him you were almost fifty—to ease the age gap. You were forty-seven then."

"I've always shaded my age up a year or two so that people will think I look younger than I am."

"You're turning fifty then," he said, not following me.

"I'll be forty-nine sooner rather than later, Lord willing," I said. *I define my age. It doesn't define me.*

"I did rob the cradle," he said. "What do you want for your birthday?"

He needed to give me something.

"Can I have anything I want?" I asked, settling back in my chair. I pulled up my knees.

My robe fell back. My legs felt good, limber. I had a slight tan. The swimming had been good for me.

He looked very tired. By an act of will he made the light come on in his eyes, and I saw him take hold. "Anything you want," he offered.

"A ride on country roads. Lunch at an awful county road diner some place where they serve apple pie and a cup of regular coffee in a thick white mug that costs fifty cents. Extended times of silence while we're riding without having to talk. I just want to look out the window and see the world go by. And then I want to eat an Early Bird dinner with wine if we want it or iced tea if we don't."

"What about a present?" he asked, growing interested. He placed both elbows on the table and cupped his chin in one hand. The trembling he was trying to hide was contained.

I peered at him over the coffee mug. He was growing less tense about the night before, and the idea that he didn't have to perform for his wife's birthday caused his shoulders to relax.

"Give me half an hour to shower, and I'll take you for a drive in the country, lunch at an awful diner where they serve apple pie and coffee. Then we can be quiet on the way home and..." He was in the middle of flirting with me when he lost his thought. He couldn't finish what he had begun to say. Disconcerted, he stood and came beside me and pressed his hand over mine. I raised it to my mouth and kissed the back of his hand, and just for a moment—a fraction of a second—he looked at me, puzzled.

"Gigi," I whispered.

And then the light came on, and he leaned down and kissed me on the mouth. He tasted of coffee and sleep and something else. Last night's wine.

"Get dressed," he said, slapping the side of my hip. "Are you losing weight?"

"Aren't you sweet," I replied automatically.

"As long as you think so we're all right."

"We're all right," I assured him.

When he had gone into his room and into his bath, I whispered after him, "It's some woman's birthday you have loved, but it's not mine."

That didn't stop us from going on a drive or finding a diner where we had ham sandwiches and apple pie that had been frozen and thawed out. The coffee was a dollar a cup. The scoop of vanilla ice cream on top of the pie was riddled with fragments of unpleasant ice, freezer burned. We drove home through winding roads and finally that same road where he had taken me that first time where the old house was decaying. I caught a quick glance of it when we drove past, and he didn't notice it.

I don't think he even remembered the house, but I did. If Faulkner's "Emily" still lived there somewhere deep inside, the poor bereaved widow had lost control of the yard. The magnolia tree had gone berserk. There were over laden unpruned branches and a yard full of blossoms no one had harvested.

The sight oddly comforted me because I was beginning to understand that my marriage wasn't unique.

23

THAT OLD FEELING

For the second night in a row, Lovejoy drank two glasses of wine with dinner, and when we got home, he wanted a third glass. He went to the small bar and the little refrigerator near it in our living room and held up the bottle: "Another?"

I did not want another one, but I said, "Sure." When you love someone, you will pretend to sip another glass of wine to keep him company.

He brought us a glass of cabernet and settled on the couch, switching on the TV and muting it while he scanned the menu of what was playing. Any old movie would please him, and he knew them all.

Restless, he couldn't make a choice and didn't ask me if something caught my eye. He just sipped and scanned, sipped and scanned, hypnotized by the flashing screen as if he were alone. But I was there. His glass of wine disappeared quickly. He refilled it. "Brighten your glass?" he inquired, coming toward me. He wobbled slightly.

"Sure," I said, though there wasn't much room in my glass. He topped it off without noticing that I had not drunk very much.

He settled down beside me, sinking closer to me and uncharacteristically kicked off his shoes. His socks had a hole in the top, and he didn't notice. It was unlike him to wear less than pristine socks. Or was it?

This was the first time that he had kicked off his shoes after dinner. He always went to his room and exchanged outside shoes for inside house slippers. I wondered if he wanted to ask me to go and get his slippers.

"You know what I like about you, Cindy?"

I couldn't have been more startled. He rarely used my real name.

"What?" I asked, pretending to sip my wine.

"You believe everything I say. Most women are very suspicious. But not you. I tell you about Marjeen and her wild oat of a mother, and you believe me."

"I believe you," I said, to keep him talking.

He leaned his head back on the sofa and settled his wine glass in his lap. It teetered, almost spilling in his lap. When he noted that, he chuckled. And then the wine spilled.

Tiredly, he leaned forward and placed the wine glass on the table. Then he stood up and unzipped his pants and pushed them down, slumping back onto the sofa. "If we don't wash these quick the wine stain won't come out."

"Stay put," I said. "I'll toss them into the washer."

"Good girl," he said, patting my fanny as I turned away from him with his pants.

When I returned, he was drinking his wine again and wanted to talk.

"Do you know what I like about you, Gigi?"

"Cindy," I said, softly. He didn't hear me.

"What?" I asked more loudly.

"You believe everything I say," he said again. "A lot of women don't—and believe me, I've known a lot of women."

"I believe you," I promised.

"I know you do. And you know what?"

"What?"

"I've made a lot of women happy. Very happy. I love every woman who loves me, and I've made every woman happy. She got her money's worth. I'll tell you that."

"I believe you," I said. He liked hearing that. I wondered if he was just using an expression about 'got her money's worth' or did he mean that literally? I wanted him to keep talking. Who was the man I had married?

He made a move to kiss me, and I stayed put. The kiss landed near my mouth, and his lips slid across my face. Pulling back, he said, "Hold still."

I did.

He kissed me hard. Then harder. Shifting his weight over me, he breathed heavily into my mouth. "Keep that breathless charm...." he said.

"You, too," I said, wriggling out from under him.

"Where you going?" he demanded.

I took his hand and pulled him to his feet.

"You're stronger than you look," he remarked.

I led him by the hand down the hallway to his room and pushed him onto his bed.

He giggled and immediately in a slow swoon that took him backwards, passed out cold with a smile on his face.

Then, I took off one of his colorful socks and the other. It was the first time I had ever seen his feet without socks. He had a sixth toe on his left foot.

He began to snore, and I took a good look at him.

He was helpless and human and tired. He had to force a twinkle in his eye, and he hid an extra toe inside an array of colorful silk socks. He considered himself a lady's man, but he was really just an ordinary man, and I was just an ordinary woman who had believed his idea of himself. I loved him differently in that moment than I had ever loved him before; and as time passed, I would think that all of the days that led up to that moment were not desire but courtship. When I covered him in the blanket, I gave my heart to him differently than I ever had before, and we were, in a way, married more truly than we had been when the preacher led us in our vows or in any of the words we had said to one another on the boat and in the car and as the other one was walking away down the hallway toward an exit or another room not shared.

I tucked the blanket snugly about him and turned off the light. Balling up his socks I took them with me to his bathroom, rinsed them out in his sink, and hung them over the towel rack.

When I took one more look at him, he had turned over, curling up almost in the fetal position. I sat beside him and placed my hand on the small of his back. I whispered to him, but he couldn't hear me, "You don't have to work so very hard for any kind of tip anymore. I'm right here, and I won't be letting you go."

I meant what I said, and if he had heard me, I wondered sadly if he would believe me.

24

YOU'D BE SO NICE
TO COME HOME TO

Soon Lovejoy was himself again. I was too.

Once a month now he scheduled a special forty-five-minute distraction which happened around 4 o'clock in the afternoon. They were pleasant minutes and all the more so I think because Lovejoy knew he could retire to his own room afterwards. I stayed in mine, relearning the pace and space of solitude that had been my companion before Lovejoy found me, courted me, wed me, and, he liked to say, had his way with me.

Afterwards sometimes I couldn't sleep. On those nights, I would go outside and swim laps in the pool under the moonlight. I liked to float on my back and look at the stars. There were times when I thought that Lovejoy was inside watching me; but if he was, he never came out to join me. When I went back in the house and crept down the hallway to my bath to shower off and put on a fresh night gown, he never seemed to hear me. He could have heard me. We were both capable, I knew, by then of not hearing the other person pass or whisper or walk or knock on one another's bedroom door.

His ways were different from time to time. He was less careful around me. I watched him less. This pace suited us both, and I was growing used to it when one day, he announced that he would be gone again—a day and a night.

Of course, I knew where he was going. I knew what he would do. The only thing I didn't know, I thought, was where he parked his little black Mercedes at The Grand and for how long he walked the boardwalk. Sat on the pier. Drank a martini toasting his memories. Lived out his idea of himself the way you practice a piece of music to try and make it just so or draw a picture until you get the light just right.

I didn't follow him. I wasn't worried. I wasn't jealous. I wasn't really even very curious.

"What are you going to do while I'm gone? Draw?"

"Perhaps," I replied. For I was sketching still. Seeing the old house had triggered the dormant impulse to catch the likeness of structures and aspects of daily life being lived. I drew doorways and windows and occasionally a child's face I had seen at the grocery store. And when he wasn't looking, I sketched Lovejoy.

I no longer felt that I didn't know the essentials about my husband. There were words I would never use out loud with my husband; but when I was talking to myself and didn't mind if God overheard, I thought of him as a gigolo. I was Gigi, and he was my gigolo. Only that word gigolo was not a harsh word at all. It was just a word, like socks is a word.

Staring up at his face, his mouth coming toward mine, that word passed across the interior landscape of my mind, and as he kissed me, I giggled.

Lovejoy

"You aren't going to ask me where I'm going?"

"I like to think of you as the mysterious Great Gatsby living a romantic elusive existence. I think of you like that. Why would I spoil it by asking you for facts?"

"Is that a compliment?" he asked, brow furrowing.

"I'll miss you," I replied simply.

His eyes brightened. "Shall I bring you a present?"

"Pralines, if they have any," I replied instantly. Once upon a honeymoon The Grand sold locally made pralines in their gift shop. They were wonderfully chewy and delicious.

That surprised him. He shrugged, not making the connection to the hotel though he had eaten one every night of our honeymoon. "I'll keep an eye out for something sweet, though the way you have lost weight I wonder that you would want to tempt yourself with the calories."

He allowed his hand to slide across my chest, patting me in a familiar affectionate way, and in that instant—with his touch, desire returned. I clasped his hand and held it, keeping him close for a few seconds more.

He waited, pleased that I was holding on. He raised my hand to his mouth and kissed the back of it with promise, his gaze holding mine.

"Sometimes it is good for us to withhold ourselves from each other. It can be very gratifying later." The first time he said that I thought it strange and irritating, but now I knew that it was just one of the ways that he paced himself.

"While you are gone, I'm going to strip down and swim naked in the pool."

The declaration startled him. Me, too. I hadn't expected to say anything other than "Be careful."

He stopped mid-step and said with one leg still in the air, "Beware of frogs."

And then my husband was gone. Just like that.

I didn't know it then, but that was the last time we would speak just that way to each other—when Frank Lovejoy was my husband and I, Cindy Louise, was his wife.

PART 3

TENDER MERCIES

Forget your troubles. C'mon, get happy
Ya better chase all your cares away
Sing Hallelujah, c'mon, get happy
Get ready for the judgment day
Harold Arlen

2 5

ONE FOR MY BABY
(AND ONE MORE FOR THE ROAD)

When the police called, I knew it was bad news. I froze. The warmth of the female voice on the other end of the line helped me to focus.

"Everything is all right, Mrs. Lovejoy, but your husband Mr. Franklin Delmar Lovejoy...."

She waited for me to confirm that he was my husband.

"Yes, he's mine, and I'm not letting him go," I declared into the receiver.

I heard the caller take a breath before continuing. "Mr. Lovejoy had an automobile accident, and he's fine. But we need you to come and help us take care of him."

She explained that Lovejoy had run off the side of the road and was in a hospital in Baldwin County. I knew the hospital. Three phone calls later, I was connected to him in a room where he was "being fiddled with," he said. Pressing his mouth close to the receiver he complained, "The women here can't keep their hands off me."

I grew stony cold, my response to danger and imminent loss.

When I reached him two and a half hours later, he was holding the remote to the TV and scanning for something to watch. His demeanor was different; and though I didn't expect a warm welcome, I thought at least he would recognize me.

My Frank didn't seem to know me at first.

Lovejoy waved me toward a chair and said, "Be with you in a minute."

Shocked, I simply ignored him. I walked on water straight to him, my legs shimmying because of the fluid flooring. I placed my hand on his hand that held the remote. Leaning over, I pressed my face against his and told him the truth, "Lovejoy. My heart."

His body grew still beneath my claim, and he sniffed my hair, his eyes closing while he remembered.

Oh, yes.

"Gigi," he said. "You were a long time coming. Too long. Oh, but you're lovely. Never, never change. Keep that breathless charm…. The way you look tonight…." He breathed, inhaling me.

"What happened, Frank?"

He breathed in and out as he collected his thoughts. And then my husband saw me and smiled truly. "It was a silly business," I confess. "I don't know why I was being so mysterious with you. I could have told you. Vanity. Vanity. All is vanity. I read that somewhere, and, boy, is it true."

"You can always tell me everything. Don't you remember? I'm the woman who believes everything you say."

He blinked, not recognizing that claim.

"I don't remember how much I told you," he admitted. "I'm not as young as I used to be. But I'm young at heart. Fairy tales can come true. It can happen to you if you're young at heart."

I blinked, trying to figure out what he meant. *Fairy tales can come true?*

I took his hand, his beautiful expressive hand. Lovejoy. Lovejoy. Inside I repeated his name. While my inner voice chanted his identity, I made small talk. "You said you were going away for a night. I thought it was one of your religious retreats." *Or you were meeting another woman for the glory of love.* That thought trailed along in the background of my resolute trust. I believe everything you say, and I wonder about you too. It is entirely possible to mean both of those ideas.

"Could you get me a drink of water?" he asked. "In the name of Jesus. Don't forget your reward," he added in a soft voice, almost to himself.

And I knew with the question that he was simply trying to move me away from him.

From the nearby brown wooden table, I retrieved the white Styrofoam cup that contained ice and water and delivered it to him. He watched his hand reach for the cup. I watched his hand reach for the cup. He was telling his hand what to do and marveling at the way his own hand moved and reached and gripped. He took a small sip of water and then another before his hand shook briefly, sloshing a few drops of water on the bed covers. He settled the cup down onto his leg and exhaled. "They don't make gin like they used to," he said, looking at me ruefully. He shrugged winsomely and added, "A little joke."

I smiled. "Do you want to tell me what happened now or do you need to rest?"

"I don't need anything but you," he replied immediately. He had hundreds of gallant expressions at the ready. Snippets of love song lyrics flowed easily from him.

Gathering his thoughts, he said, "It is entirely silly and vain of me I know, but I signed up for a talent contest at a tavern not far from here, and, well, I was just wondering if I still had *it*. Do you know how you wonder if you still have *it*? Vanitas. Vanitatum. Someone said that once, and boy, is it true. Vanitatum."

I studied my sweet lover in the hospital bed with wires attached to him and a monitor that occasionally flashed a jagged red line across a screen. I perched on the bed beside him and felt the outline of his leg. The weight of his body comforted me, and I would have crawled under the sheets with him and held him close if there hadn't been so many strangers nearby. I told him none of this, for there is a season inside a marriage when you can say words like that to your husband; but as time passes, you must retreat from the activity of avowing passion and intense everlasting love. I asked quietly, "What do you mean by *it* exactly?"

He cleared his throat and sat up straighter as a male aide wearing beige thermal knit underwear under a set of light blue perma-pressed scrubs asked, "Did you ever get warm, Franklin?"

Lovejoy placed a hand over his heart and replied, "Warm as can be. Thanking you."

The short stocky aide who had short curly brown hair and Mickey Mouse ears offered a thumbs up, and cast a quick questioning glance at me: *who are you*?

"Mrs. Lovejoy," I replied to his raised eye brows.

He offered a wave and said brightly more to Lovejoy than to me: "Toodles."

Once the aide had left, Lovejoy couldn't remember what he was about to say.

"What did you mean by still having *it*? What is *it*?"

"I used to sing. I've told you that much. People used to like to hear me sing."

"The ladies," I interjected.

"And I was let go before I was finished singing is what happened. I've been doing all kinds of things since then, but I just wondered if I could still sing. I didn't want you to see me fail. That's why I didn't tell you about it. Vanitas, vanitatum. All is vanity. Somebody said that once, and, boy, were they right. I think it was Mark Twain or somebody like that. Yes, vanity, vanity, all is vanity."

"You didn't fail," I theorized softly, shifting back on the bed as a nurse pushing a machine strolled past. "It's a busy place," I said, to fill the silence.

"Yes, and I'm the most popular man here. They come and go. If the people who worked here had been in the tavern, I would have gotten much more applause and come in first place instead of third. I came in third place. There were 8 people, almost 9. One got stage fright and left. There was no money involved except the entrance fee—sixty-five dollars. That includes a dinner for two and a bottle of wine. I suffered many congratulations! I suffered; I'll tell you. I drank the wine, and then I headed home. I shouldn't have been driving because I had been drinking and, well, you should know, I flirted a bit with the ladies. But to be perfectly honest with you the ladies expect it. Ladies do it to themselves eventually."

"You have a way with the ladies." I sat down on the side of his bed, and I looked around the room for a sign of his clothes—his colored socks and feared that the worst had happened. They had taken away his camouflage socks and left his poor feet and that sad sixth toe exposed under the covers for any nurse or technician to see. I resolved to buy him socks as soon as I could.

"My way with the ladies is a gift from God, and I've tried to use it for his glory," he said, soberly. "And my car went off the side of the road, and I landed here. I guess I've still got some of it after all just not as much, maybe." He sighed, handing me his cup of water. He rubbed the side of his face thoughtfully. "I need a shave. When I get home, I'll shave first thing."

"Are you hurt?"

"My pride. I'm going to be out of action for a while my dear, and for that I deeply apologize."

I waved aside his apology, placing my hand on the top of his thigh. He eyed it thoughtfully, and for a second, I thought he didn't know why I should be able to place my hand there. Right there. I removed it, and his shoulders relaxed. That was the first time in all the time that I knew and was married to my husband when I realized that deep down my Frank was shy. He camouflaged his shyness with good clothes and fine manners, but he was shy. Who but God knew what being a ladies' man had cost him? He fidgeted with his hands, clasping them self-consciously, finally in his lap.

"What song did you sing that won you third prize?"

"My signature song. Old Blue Eyes and I sing it. Sang it. Did Sinatra die? You know Frank, the Chairman of the Board." Lovejoy began to sing softly to himself, "Make it one for my baby and one more for the road…. Maybe it was "My Funny Valentine." All the best love songs are kind of the same. I was myself-- wistful and romantic. They aimed one small spotlight on me while I sat on a stool the way Frank did when he sang, "Set 'em up Joe…." Lovejoy hummed some more, his head leaning back against the two pillows that had been bunched up behind him. His mouth quivered suddenly, and I reached out and took both his hands in mine. He didn't seem to feel me do that, and we sat there like that, his head back, his eyes closed, my hands on top of both of his, frozen in time and space like a rest note in a piece of music that will resume but not yet. Not yet.

When he roused, I planned to ask Lovejoy why he wouldn't sing a whole song for me all the way through.

But before I could say another word or ask another question, a knock on the door interrupted us. It was the police, two officers in uniform, but only the woman held a piece of paper.

"I'm Mrs. Lovejoy, and this is my husband," I said, rising, placing my body between her and my husband in the hospital bed.

She smiled at me. It was a friendly smile—not a policeman smile, not a judge's smile, not even a female polite smile. It was a smile I knew very well. It was a Southern woman's smile—a magnolia smile, beaming, honest and forgiving. She smiled at me warmly; and as soon as she did, I thought, *you'd make a great Christian*, but I didn't say that to her.

"This is a copy of the accident report which you will need."

She told me where Frank's car had been towed.

"Looked totaled to me," she said. And then with a nod of her head toward the doorway she led me to where her partner was waiting for her, his black eyes as warm and friendly as his partner's, and that surprised me. "Ma'am, alcohol was involved in the problem with the car, but my best advice—my solemn best advice—is that you don't let him drive anymore. Take away his car keys before he hurts someone other than himself next time."

"This is his first accident. He can drive."

"Ma'am, just think about it. Once alcohol and age are documented like this in an accident, you can be held liable if someone else gets hurt," she said, as her partner received a message on a device plugged into his ear. He signaled to her that they needed to leave.

It's strange to bid two police officers good-bye with affection, but I felt so very warmly toward them. They had helped my Frank—protected him from himself without judging him or me. I wanted to walk them to the door, to tell them, *thank you for coming, come again*, but the niceties of Southern womanhood did not fit the farewell. I watched them walk down the hallway, and some part of me that liked to murmur in the background of my life whispered, "Keep them safe and as wonderful as they are today," and I lingered there inside that unbidden, whispered honest prayer while my husband nodded off.

I sat down in a chair beside the window and let the sun bake the tensions out of me. Time passed. I do not know how much time. But when my Lovejoy awoke, he broke immediately into a ready smile, and said, "Hello, you."

*****

It would be two days before I could get him home and find out about Frank's car. It was totaled. He didn't seem to mind or mourn. When I tried to talk with him about it, he said quietly, "It was only metal. Only a car. To aliens it would have been a gizmo. A baby's rattle. Something like that."

By then he was more himself than he had been in the hospital and oddly removed from the trauma of the accident or the surprise of only coming in third with his signature song.

He had taken to humming Frank Sinatra's "One for my Baby," and I knew that he wasn't humming to me. In his way, in his mind, he might have been practicing for the next time when he would attempt a comeback. Or maybe it was his way of praying a heart full of love.

"I'll be my old self again in no time," he promised; but he was wrong.

He never would be his old self again, and I never would be my old self again. The difference was that I knew it, and I didn't mourn about the changes happening in both of us.   Day after day, we changed, becoming strangers in the night off and on but never for very long.

26

I CAN'T GIVE YOU
ANYTHING BUT LOVE

"It's so much easier to manage a woman if you know how to distract her," he said, as if I weren't sitting beside him listening to him talk to himself.

But I was. We watched "Gaslight" with Charles Boyer and Ingrid Bergman.

'Poor Ingrid. She suffers so,' I thought.

At the conclusion, Lovejoy said one thing, his hands at first open as if he were about to clap, but no, he didn't clap. He said, "He did it the hard way," and then he pressed his hands together like a prayer.

The movie that followed was "Midnight Lace" starring Doris Day. "I met Doris Day once," Lovejoy said. "Doris Day. Not exactly the girl next door, if you know what I mean. But then none of them were, really. Rosemary Clooney. June Allyson. Not the girls next door that you are supposed to think of when you hear that phrase—not by a long shot."

"I don't know what you mean," I said.

"She was taller than you expect her to be. Doris. Nice smile, Doris. You can walk a million miles on a nice smile. I know that."

We turned off the movie about a third of the way into it. "Dumb. Dumb. Dumb," he said.

I didn't know. I hadn't really been paying attention. I was sketching Lovejoy on a small white pad I had bought with a package of black ink pens designed for drawing. I found myself trying to catch his expressions, the light landing on him, the shape of his hands on the table, then his lap, around a cup. Once he looked up and said in a strong voice very clearly, "You can't catch who I am without you in the picture. We are lovers," he said. "Married lovers. Nothing more. Nothing less. You have to put yourself in the picture with me, or what you're trying to draw can never be true. Not true!" He shook his head for emphasis.

I smiled and kept drawing. He was such a sweet talker. I liked the way his mouth looked when he said those words, and I tried to draw a picture of it. Soon I had filled my little pad of paper with quick sketches of him. Five days into his recovery I was on the verge of developing carpal tunnel syndrome from drawing Lovejoy when he said, "You're like that photographer taking pictures of that old house. Do you remember that old house?"

The question caused me to stop. Lovejoy hadn't paid any attention to that house when we had recently passed it. He walked over to me and placed his hand on the pad of paper covering the picture I was drawing of him. When my eyes met his, he entreated, "Enough. I'm not changing that fast, and I'm not dying. At least I don't think I'm dying today. You don't need to be in a hurry to store me up or save the way you see me. Write me a letter if you must. I'll read it. Women love to write me love letters."

"Is that what I'm doing?" I wondered aloud. Were my sketches love letters that used images instead of words?

He leaned over and kissed me the way he had on our first date, and my body leaned back and away from him while my heart yearned toward him at the same time.

He didn't notice. "I'm going to read my mail."

I drew a picture of him leaving me, walking down the ill-lit hallway shoeless, wearing the yellow socks with the non-skid tabs on them he had brought home from the hospital.

After his first flutter, which is what Frank called his car accident, he didn't seem to remember to wear his special socks anymore.

******

Three weeks after his accident, on a Sunday morning, I was five minutes late getting dressed for church even though I was having a good hair day. I was moving slowly, at the pace of remembered love. We had made love the night before. My skin looked rosy, and I felt satisfied, even though I shouldn't have. Lovejoy held the door, shaking his head, "I hope no one else has gotten our pew. You know how I like to sit where we sit. Because we've missed the last two weeks somebody else might have gotten our seat."

No one had.

In fact, we received quite a welcome with lots of hugs and teasing. "We've been on a second honeymoon," he bragged. "Anniversary. Three years. Time flies when you are in love."

I had every reason to believe that he believed what he was saying. That idea made believing him easier.

He was especially pleased with himself, taking the church bulletin that would lead us through the worship service. We only took one to share. *Waste not. Want not.* Today, Lovejoy held onto the church bulletin, smiling, nodding, steering.

An announcement for the next Missions Conference was on the pew waiting for us—waiting for everyone. I always thought it was strange to put out so many announcements on pews where people sit. Wasn't there a better way to remind people about dates and special events? I mean—you have to come to church to find the announcement, and if you are coming to church, don't you know?

I had said those words once to someone in charge, and he had not replied—just walked away, shaking his head while he prayed, "Lord have mercy. Lord have mercy."

A lot of people have prayed that after they spoke with me about church work.

There were two announcements about the Missions Conference, and Lovejoy studied both with intense interest. Then he reached over and patted my hand consolingly. "They didn't choose your verse for the conference brochure. Don't lose heart," Lovejoy whispered. "There's always next year."

I didn't know what Frank meant at first. I had not submitted a verse this year for the Missions Conference. I had sent in a verse for the past two years as possible slogans after

Lovejoy nagged me for days about it. But JD and the other powers-that-be had not chosen either of my proposed verses for a conference motto—no reason to try again this year. 'Once a loser at church always a loser at church.' That's how I thought about it.

I read the verse selected for this year. It was a regular old Bible verse about 'Go make disciples of the nations.' The conference verse is usually something like that. The conference song usually rotates from "Send the Light, the Blessed Gospel Light" to "Go Tell It on the Mountain". I like "Go Tell It on the Mountain" better, so I anonymously suggested a song that was kind of like that song for the conference theme song, but my recommendation is not a Christian song per se. That is a very tricky business in a church—a tight rope few people dared to walk. But I dared! I had dropped my recommendation for the Missions Conference theme song anonymously into the suggestion box. I figured if I had signed my name it would have immediately gone to the trash can, so I didn't sign it. I just wrote the title of the song and the first verse. "Get Happy. Drop all your worries, come on, get happy. Get ready for the Judgment Day." And then because I was in a sketching mood, I drew a little picture of some dancing feet with the little numbers that pointed them to that Bible verse about gospel breathers having beautiful feet. Something like that, only I don't think the Bible calls evangelists gospel breathers.

My feet began to move just thinking about singing the song that Judy Garland had made famous. I had heard her sing it in one of those old movies Lovejoy made me watch on Sunday afternoons. That was the day he told me Judy Garland started out as Frances Gumm and was part of an act. The Gumm Sisters or The Gumdrops?

Before I could brag to him—and I thought finally, thank you, Jesus, make my husband proud of me, too! -- that the powers-that-be had picked my proposed song for this year's conference and apparently used my illustration of dancing feet as the logo artwork too, Lovejoy read the selected Missions Conference theme song title in the church bulletin. His face grew stern, his brow furrowed. Then, just as quickly, Frank made his expression go neutral as then he whispered in my ear: "Somebody's lost their mind. "Get Happy" is a Judy Garland song, and she was a slut of the first order."

He leaned closer and whispered in my ear louder than he needed to say the words, "Judy started out as a member of a duet called the Gummy Bears—something like that—but she changed her name; and all her life long, blame it on the drugs or men, say what you will, she was a tramp. Actually, there are worse words for what she was, but I won't use them in church."

Shrugging, I replied simply, "Life happens." That was as close as I could get to having a 'love thy neighbor' response without quoting the exact Bible verse.

His shoulders dropped then. A sigh escaped him, and for a second, I wished I had asked him to wear his Point Clear hat to church, the straw hat with the black band. That hat always gave Frank such confidence when he needed strength. The hat hung in the hallway now, but he didn't seem to see it.

Lovejoy

I was missing the man who sat out on the pier thinking of himself as a mysterious man like Gatsby when suddenly Lovejoy's hand failed him. The hymnal which he had been holding for us both dropped, hitting the floor because I wasn't holding it too. Then, my Lovejoy slumped, falling back on the pew.

The service which had only barely begun with a musical interlude that called people to worship continued; but the pianist, sensitive to a change in tempo in the sanctuary and to the hand motion of the preacher who waved for her to continue also signaled to a deacon to help us at our pew. The congregation grew quiet, and a doctor whose specialty was broken knees, feet, and hips came over and assessed Lovejoy solemnly, taking his pulse and nodding: "His heart's still beating. He's just not quite with us." And before I knew what was happening, two other deacons appeared, lifted my husband, and took him out of the sanctuary so that the service could go on while we waited for the ambulance.

Woodenly, I followed the deacons out the side door to a classroom near the exit where Lovejoy had first waited for me that Wednesday night when I told myself he was just flirting with me. He wasn't flirting with me now. He was somewhere else, and I knew that. Knew it differently than I had ever known anything about anyone, including myself.

My Lovejoy was out on the boat in the bright winter sunlight now standing there in his shorts and feeling the sun and the bite of cold and living inside the presence of God himself. That's what I knew. He was poised inside the kind of love and joy that he had met one afternoon on a boat and he had been keeping company there off and on for a while now. That's what I knew, and while I knew it there were tears expressing life's sorrows trailing down my face.

The preacher showed up by my side, leaving the congregation during the singing of opening hymns to do what preachers do: come alongside someone who is about to suffer a great loss or a great change or…. die and leave a lot of money to the church. (I wish I didn't think thoughts like that, but I do.)

That thought did come to me, and later I edited that refrain from my memory of the moment.

Later, I just recalled the preacher's hand on the middle of my back and the universal pat of reassurance, twice: *There, there. It will be all right.*

Sometimes that's all anyone can do or say—even a preacher. I remember thinking that, too.

And then Lovejoy and I were transported to the hospital, where they called what happened to him a light stroke or a light heart attack. They weren't sure. They ran tests, but the results were inconclusive. I remember the expressionless faces of the experts who told me that "It was something unusual. An aberration. Hard to diagnose. Whatever it was, he had some kind of episode. He needs to rest. So, do you."

Later Lovejoy would call his episode, "A flutter. I had myself another flutter. They happen like bird wings in flight— little flutters while you're flying." His words were inscrutable, but his message was clear to me. He was somewhere else in the flutter, and in a way that only marriage can make sense of, because we were one, I was with him. I would always be with him. He would never let me go. I would never let him go. Yet we would live apart in all the ways that people do live apart. And be together.

His smile was different now, and the gaze in his eyes was childlike and trusting. The experts don't know how to write down the differences in gazes and smiles on their charts and call it data. Only people who love the one who had the flutter see those changes, and we don't have anyone to tell. Not that many people listen to you anyway once you become a caregiver. That's what I became. Once upon a time I was Cindy, then I was Gigi. At the same time, I was Mrs. Lovejoy, and then I became a caregiver. Of all of those identities the one who got the most pats on the back and the intended refrain of *there, there* was the caregiver role, but the pats on the back weren't always encouragement. They were like, *gotta run, gotta scoot, gotta go, see ya later, tough luck, hang in there, pray on, ask Jesus to help you, He will.*

There was a difference in Frank's speech—not articulation or word choice. The change didn't fit what they call a symptom. He was slower. Church ladies say this among themselves with the gentle admission about their beloveds: "My husband's winding down."

My Lovejoy and he was surely mine now and no one else's, and yes, that idea did pulse through me and was comforting, was slow to speak, slow to answer, slow to frame replies to simple questions. I could say, "How are you?" and fifteen minutes later or longer, my Frank would turn his head, turn his head just so at an angle that seemed uncomfortable, and frame the words of his reply, "Lovely to be here, don't you know?"

I wondered if that answer was from some old song he used to sing, but I didn't recognize it, and he didn't hum it.

He couldn't walk like himself for a long while, but it wasn't because he couldn't. He just didn't want to walk anymore. His eyes frequently leaked with unrestrained tears. He wasn't sobbing. He wasn't in pain. He wasn't crying. Old love songs were draining from his ocean blue eyes. That's what it looked like to me. I couldn't describe in words what I was seeing, so I continued to draw more and more.

He let tears flow, and I drew them. Sometimes I cried, too.

I became the only person who could write the checks. That's when I learned how much money he had and how much of mine he had spent.

It was a rude awakening.

27

MY FUNNY VALENTINE

F riends from church organized food deliveries and other "we're just checking on you" visits to break up the monotony of being housebound. Susan and Judy came together, bringing that chicken spaghetti dish that the church stores up in round tins for people to grab and deliver in the name of Jesus. They also brought a key lime pie. The pie was very good.

But Lovejoy didn't eat much of either one. I did. I was ferociously hungry, and though I initially thought I wouldn't like people bringing food to the house, I ate it all because I needed my strength.

Caregiving is a full-time job. And the man I thought I knew became a fresh mystery to me.

He grew bored quickly. It took him two hours to read the newspaper and an hour for us to get him bathed and dressed. Then, one day after we had mastered this slow routine, he said in that new way of speaking that I had learned to understand: "I want to go on a mission trip."

I shook my head. "Oh, darlin'…." I began before he stopped me from saying anything else.

He fixed a gaze on me and repeated. "I must live my life. Take me to that Respite Center over at the Methodist church for people like me who need help and want to give help. That's what the story says. They need volunteers. People need to give and to receive no matter what shape they're in. That's the gospel I know, and that's my mission field now. I shall volunteer."

"I don't know what you mean."

He pointed to a story in the local newspaper about a senior citizen Respite ministry for people who had different challenges in their lives. He was very sure about it.

So, I called and talked to the lady in charge, who spoke to me very slowly on the telephone. "It's not for me," I explained. "It's for my husband."

"Respite is for you both," she replied, and I could feel her smile through the telephone. I liked her instantly and made an appointment to meet her and see the gathering room where neighbors visit with each other in the name of Jesus. After the tour, she walked me to my car and stopped under an ancient magnolia tree. We instinctively sat down in the shade to feel the breeze and visit.

That's what I called it later. Visited. Afterwards, I told Lovejoy all about her, and he listened to me, but I don't think he understood what I said, and it didn't matter. "She's a sweet girl with a great personality, and I think you'll love getting to know her and her friends."

That wasn't the whole truth. Once that sweet girl waved a hand for me to sit a spell under her magnolia tree, I started talking and I couldn't stop. I told her everything that I had been feeling, and she just patted my hand and said, "I know. I know. We all know here what life is like. It's hard and wonderful. It's brutal and kind. It's inspiring and it's tragic."

I nodded and nodded and fought the urge to crawl over onto a small patch of sunlight on the ground and curl up like a cat and go to sleep at her feet while she shooed the flies away. She seemed to know I was thinking about that, and she said, "You can get some rest while we keep your husband company. And he'll keep us company. It's a radical kind of friendship. We all just love each other to bits here."

After I had gushed to Lovejoy for a while about how much I liked that girl and what she said, he replied simply, "I'm the one who told you about it. Enough with the talking. Let's just go."

The first time I delivered Lovejoy to Respite, two men were standing outside waiting to welcome him and shepherd him to the room where the doors had locks. Once you went inside you couldn't wander out again without a volunteer beside you or your loved one.

That troubled me, and then it comforted me, and then I drove over to a local spa and paid an enormous amount of money to sit in their Quiet Room and listen to the water fall in the corner. With four hours of private time, I went next to the heated wading pool and soaked with my head back on a rolled towel. From there I went to the steam room where I drew up my legs and sweated. Then I showered, got a pedicure and drank a mimosa while my toenails dried with that special mauve polish which I had never been able to find before. The spa girl applied it twice to my nails after my heels had been oompahed. Is that a word? That's what she said. She oompahed my heels with a hard sponge. It kind of hurt, and I kind of liked it.

I didn't always go to the spa on the days Lovejoy went to Respite. Actually, I only went to the spa that first day, and then I didn't go again until Christmas. During the intervening days, I learned to drop off Lovejoy at the side door of the Methodist church, and two people—not always the same people-- welcomed him every day, and I learned how to be alone again but in a different way. Part of learning that was watching Lovejoy leave with the two welcoming volunteers. That's how I thought about them. The volunteers steered my sweetheart into the building and waved at me to *Go on, he will be all right. We'll take care of him for you.*

I learned to trust them, and they were trustworthy. Lovejoy thrived there. He got stronger. He even seemed to become more alert for longer periods of time, but I also learned that what we think of as being alert isn't as valuable as we believe human accomplishment or human reasoning should be. He seemed to love others more than he ever had, and so did I.

So, while he was at Respite, I did all kinds of things.

I ran errands.

Got my hair done.

Did the shopping.

Checked on the banking business.

Sometimes I even washed my car after gassing it up, because taking Lovejoy to the gas station was awful. He wanted to help so badly, and he couldn't work the pump.

Lovejoy

I used my time efficiently and, strangely, lived my life luxuriantly while Lovejoy was volunteering at Respite. I let him have his private life. People forget that in whatever state you are in you need some kind of private life. Part of that private life came to me under the magnolia tree where I waited when I arrived early to pick him up. There I got to know other people just like me (that was a shock!) who were waiting on their lovejoys.

Out under the magnolia trees I sat with the other spouses while their loved ones were inside playing games and singing songs and eating a hot meal that had two desserts. I met an older woman who was waiting for her husband just like I was. She liked to talk about the past and her children, and her memories were love songs that just weren't set to music. I halfway listened; and while she spoke, I felt like humming along, but I didn't.

"I used to sit like this when my daughter Katie was in school, and I was waiting outside for her." She stared off toward a stand of trees at the end of the grounds. Beyond that was a place—a direction where her child had grown up. She could go there in a heartbeat now.

Her voice was sweet the way an angel sounds, the one who whispers in your ear while you sleep.

She kind of crooned: "I always went early to pick Katie up so I could have the thrill of seeing her come out the school door—to see the expression on her face before she fixed her expression to meet me, her mama, and that's what I was to her: her mama. But if I got there early, I could see the face Katie wore with the world, and I loved seeing that face and storing the memory of it because it was the face that told the truest truth about who she was—not manufactured or remembered in response to her mama. And day after day, year after year, I got to meet my child by watching her face come out the school's door as she grew up by herself on the other side, and I would store the memory of her growing up like that and how she fixed her face to come to me and get inside and stare glumly out the window, and I remember wondering what kind of face I wore for her—what kind of expression did I fix on my face so that she wouldn't know that I was thrilled...thrilled....to see her? Mamas love their children in ways children can't bear because it is so intense, and we have to hide it. And we love our husbands intensely too, but he gets to see that when he can bear to be loved that much. The deep fervor of our love gets expressed in all kinds of ways, and it sometimes pours out. You just don't figure after fifty years that you can grow in your love and that you will, with a start of joy upon seeing the face that comes to you after just a few hours of being with strangers, that he will have changed— but he still comes to you, and the difference between a husband and a child is that he is less guarded, less fixed, and even though my love's face is frozen on one side, I know his eyes well enough to see the start of joy, the thrill that still exists between us. Is that how it is with you and Mr. Lovejoy?"

"Yes," I said readily in a voice that almost sounded like who I am. Gone were the fears, suspicions, doubts, jealousy and interpreting Lovejoy's need for privacy as a rejection of me. He has loved me the way he loves me, and I love him the way I love him. "That's how it is for me. Frank thrills me."

Lovejoy

The doors opened, and slowly our loves came out and to us through the shadows and under the over laden limbs of ancient trees older than Faulkner or Fitzgerald, Emily or Gatsby. "And there he comes."

Frank came out with a helpful lady on either side, and he looked old. I didn't know he was old. I never knew Lovejoy was old. But he was most likely old when I fell in love with him.

He had grown older.

He had used me in the name of love.

Robbed me in the name of tender mercies.

And I loved him so.

2 8

AS TIME GOES BY

"Your husband is such a flirt," the afternoon volunteer told me one day. "And he has a beautiful voice. Your Lovey sang for us today. We had a piano player. One of the volunteers."

It was a beautiful day really. My heart was broken, and it was a beautiful day. That's what a caregiver learns. You can have both ideas like that inside yourself and mean them both. I looked up at Lovejoy and his two new girlfriends—both of whom had the same name: Volunteer. That's what their tags said, and I thought it a beautiful, beautiful universal name for which I had never heard a love song written, but someone should write a love song for volunteers, I know that. I asked as if Frank weren't standing right there beside them, "Does he sing often?"

"This was the first time. I'm Vivi, by the way."

(Yes, I thought, Vivi would be a nickname for a volunteer who wore her eyebrows turned up at the corners like that.)

"But it won't be his last, we hope." Vivi patted Frank's arm through which she had looped her hand, and I saw him press his arm against her midriff in response. I knew that move of his. He has a way of getting close to you that you would have minded in someone else but not him. Vivi picked up his hand

and moved it toward me. "Here's your Lovey. He ate some. Not much."

There was no judgment or advice intended in that statement. It was just relevant news now. I nodded. His appetite hadn't been very good since his most recent flutter. And he often went into frozen states—immobilized postures as if he were thinking deeply about something. When that happened, I always saw him out on that boat that he had described where he had met God under the too-bright sun and when the air was cool and the water had some chop to it. *I felt alive. So alive.* He had told me. Yes, that's what I thought his frozen states were, and I share them from time to time when it won't invade his privacy.

But they were not happening as frequently as before he had started his season at the Respite center. Something good was happening to him there. Now, he was singing again. He was popular. The ladies liked him, and I wasn't jealous—not even a little bit.

The next time I made it a point to arrive early, and though I understood that he still needed his privacy and I valued my time, I slipped into the back of the big gathering room and watched the movements of the people inside: the clients and the volunteers. I couldn't tell the volunteers from the clients, but I did see the piano at the far end of the room and the chairs had been stationed around it. It wasn't a grand piano. It was a brown spinet about a hundred years old.

They were all singing at first, and the person leading the music was using hand motions.

"Exercise," I saw. Chair calisthenics. Oh, my.

Lovejoy

The clients went through the motions with two songs, and then the music stopped, and the lady I had met that first time and who ran the group called my husband, "Lovey."

I couldn't remember her name. That bothered me at first, and then it didn't.

She called my Lovejoy Lovey, but he didn't react.

The leader tried a different tact, changing the modulation of her voice and going over to stand in front of him. His cane was centered in front of him between his two legs, which had gotten thin. He needed to eat more, but it was hard to tempt him.

"Franklin, do you feel like singing today?" she asked for the second time. She was sweet, pacing herself to meet his pace of hearing and reacting.   Her voice reached him this time.

"For you, always, my dear," he said, rising slowly, gallantly, and going to her as she extended her hand. He made his way slowly with the cane while the piano player eased into a tune.

"I love a Gershwin tune," Lovejoy promised. "Or anything."

"The Way You Look Tonight," someone called.

"My Funny Valentine. Sing "My Funny Valentine."

The throng of people murmured among themselves then.

Lovejoy was right.   His generation requested the same songs whether they were on a cruise ship or at a meeting of people who struggled with various ailments or infirmities. Sometimes they gathered because they had outlived everyone else and needed a new circle of people to love.

I looked around the room at all the people who belonged to someone else; but in that moment, they were there as themselves, perfectly single, alone in the stage of life that had brought them here, and there was my Lovejoy smiling, his now silver hair combed well though it lacked a luster that it used to have when he chose his own hair products. He looked clean. He had on his seersucker suit and a bow tie that matched his lemon-yellow socks, which I had helped him to put on. He no longer asked for his special socks or really needed them.

I'm the one who wanted him to wear his special socks for old time's sake. Neither one of us noticed his sixth toe anymore. He wasn't self-conscious, and I didn't count it. Wasn't surprised. Didn't see it as a defect. Didn't even feel sorry for him. It was just an extra toe. A spare. Maybe God thought a man who had a way with the ladies needed an extra toe the way the Apostle Paul who had seen a special view of heaven had been assigned a humbling thorn in his side to keep him humble.

My husband was singing before I could hear him. I saw his mouth move. Then, realizing that the room couldn't hear him, the Boss—that's what her name tag said, held the microphone for him. He sang and sang, his ocean blue gaze roaming around the room with his eyes smiling naturally—not from will or habit or to earn tips. His gaze while singing was the same as that first time when I had really looked into his eyes, which were the color of the old South, blue-grey. The light in his eyes was a show of honest delight to be present in their company.

"My funny Valentine. Sweet comic Valentine. You make me smile with my heart. Your looks are laughable. Unphotographable. Yet, you're my favorite work of art. Is your figure less than Greek?"

He still had *it*. He sang on with a voice I had never heard in him before, but it was there in that moment. When the crowd applauded, he bowed. Gallantly. It must have been his signature bow from years ago on the cruise ship.

Frank made his way to his chair without knowing I was there, without seeing me. He sat between two women, both of whom patted an arm. A woman behind him reached out and stroked the back of his neck. He turned and offered her a knowing smile. He had a way with the ladies.

And that's when he saw me, but he didn't recognize me. His eyes went right over —didn't stop.

I rose and waved, but he turned and faced the Boss, who asked if someone else would like to sing. This time a woman rose and took the microphone and led them in a crowd-pleaser (that's what she called it) "Down by the old mill stream, where I first met you...." The woman had *it*, just like Frank had *it*. Everyone who sang had *it* too.

They sang that song and then another one as the circle of neighbors positioned around the piano dwindled when members of their families arrived and tapped them on the shoulders, signaling it was time to go home.

One by one the members of the group rose and went off with the person who had come to collect them—spouses, siblings, professional caregivers collecting the person who needed caregiving, and I waited—watched—didn't grieve, wondered when Lovejoy would grow restless and start looking for me, but he never did. If I hadn't been inside, they would have escorted him out to me, but that day was different: I joined him. Them. I was one of them after all, which is the heart message of the Respite Ministry, I think. Everyone is welcome. Everyone belongs.

Finally, when both ladies on either side of him had been collected and the lady behind him had kissed him one final time on the back of his head while patting his shoulder, I walked around to my sweetheart and smiled. Frank looked up expectantly—he always expected affection. I hope he saw it in my eyes. For the love I knew now was much deeper and richer than the passion of first desire. This love was different. I was born to love like this, and he had been my lover and still was in the truest sense.

Did he see my love for him by then? I do not know the answer.

Most often, I saw confusion in his eyes and a docile willingness to be led home. Though I took his crooked elbow and moved with him toward the door, it was I steering us to our car that I alone now drove. We had never bought a replacement for the black sports car. The subject had never come up.

When we got home, he needed to rest, and I needed wine. He curled up on the sofa, and I threw a wrap over him. I poured a glass of wine and watched the clock strike the hour of the Early Bird dinner, but he and I would not be going out for that. Those were our good old days. We had three years or so of good old days.

I peeled off my clothes and went outside in my underwear as I had a long time ago and dived into the pool and began to swim the laps that eased the tension that ran through my body. I no longer swam naked. I just swam, building my strength because I would need to be as strong as possible for longer than I knew.

A half hour later I dried off and came inside, and Frank was waking up and pushing up on the couch and looking through the shadows.

"Is it time?" he asked.

"It's always time," I replied, ruffling his hair.

"Do we have enough?" he asked, taking a deep breath.

"We have enough," I assured him. I would have asked him if he were hungry but he could not manage questions upon waking. Instead, I said: "Dinner will be ready soon."

"Baked fish and peas?" he asked. His voice was hopeful.

During these days he wanted baked fish and peas.

"If that's what you want," I replied simply.

"Anything at all—as long as I'm with you, Cynthia."

He had stopped calling me Gigi, and I was glad. So very glad.

Marjeen came to visit twice, bringing her three-year old son named Francis, and I wrote her a check, which she didn't question—just eyed Lovejoy, curiously, and me with a suspicion that she could never name.

I watched the bank balance grow less and less as time passed, and sometimes when Lovejoy asked me if we had enough and I said yes, I wondered if I was telling the truth. He always believed me.

29

STAR DUST

We buried Lovejoy in his family plot, a piece of ground I discovered after I went through his desk just after he became bedridden and quiet. Very quiet. The house was even quieter after he was gone. I missed his humming and the sound of him moving about in his room and the rush of water from his bathroom tap when he rinsed out his socks and the first fifteen minutes of drip-drip-drip after his socks began to hang dry but had to lose water first. He never really wrung out the socks as well as he might have.

This small lack of skill he had in reference to his sock washing was nothing. Just nothing. As are other habits of living, being, and doing that require little conversation and no discussion. So much of living doesn't require judgment or discussion. So much of living can be summed up in a held hand and a love song. I learned that in the four and half years I was married to Franklin Delmar Lovejoy.

As I said we buried him in the plot of family land. Darla and Amanda were buried there and because there was an empty space between them, I nodded, yes, that may do for me one day.

Perhaps I will be with them all one day too. It is hard to say, and I don't have a preference.

It was Amanda's Country Club membership Lovejoy had inherited, but the house had originally belonged to Darla. Both were mine now. As I backtracked through his possessions, it became clear that the women he had loved and who had loved him had supported him and what I concluded was his cause in life—his mission. To love the ladies and introduce them to the love of God who appreciated their unlovable parts as we, I'm sure, one by one saw that that sixth toe of his was imminently forgettable.

If he were to describe my unlovable parts I don't know what he would say, exactly. He never said anything really that could have been a rejection. More often it was a kindly meant rebuke. In the gentlest way he knew, he simply remarked, "Your words can sound a little harsh" and "We mustn't hoard our possessions" and "What do you have that wasn't given to you by someone else so why do you think that missionaries shouldn't be supported by churches?"

I don't know what he would have said to me over time if we had had more time together. All I had left were the love songs he hummed and the ones he spoke: A your adorable. B you're beautiful C.... One of these days I will have to look up all the words to that alphabet song that was Lovejoy's go-to tribute to me and I suspect so many others. He loved us all. I believe that.

At the funeral Judy and Susan came over to pay their condolences. They were crying softly, and I wasn't—not that day in that moment, and the truth was it would take a long time before all the tears for Lovejoy emerged. In that moment they each took a hand of mine and said the words Southern women give to each other from their hearts, their earlier warning about him gone and forgotten: "He was special."

"He loved me," I testified.

"Of course he did."

"So much," Susan said.

They both meant it. They were both polite. They were both headed to a more fun lunch after the funeral, and for a second—just a second—I wanted to sing Lovejoy's alphabet song to them—to tell them what he had convinced me was true. All my aspects were lovable. Theirs were too. When you learn that and can believe it, the experience of that love changes you.

Lovejoy's love changed me. With no one at home to talk to, I began to say "Amen" out loud to the preacher on Sunday mornings when I agreed with him, and I agreed with him most Sundays. After a while my amens, an echoing love song bequeathed to me by my lover, caused other people to start speaking up, agreeing with the preacher more and more so that I was almost drowned out by it. Eventually my amens existed mostly inside myself with the memories of Lovejoy and Gatsby and Faulkner, all figures of beauty and mystery and perhaps even romance.

My drawing ceased, however. It happened after the preacher came for his follow-up bereavement visit. He brought an earnest young deacon with him—someone who was learning the routine of condolence calls. I didn't mind. I stopped minding the appearance of interns and trainees after the dermatologist examined me while a young intern from India observed. Later when I was in a dentist's chair, a college student observed in the corner. It took me a while to realize that I have reached the age when professionals identify me as someone who won't mind sacrificing my privacy to help a younger person get the intern training or on-the-job experience required to do the work of their chosen profession. So, it didn't surprise me to meet a new deacon, Hubert Reeves.

Hubert couldn't decide whether to smile or look sad, because this was a condolence call. He took a seat right beside the preacher on the sofa where you can see the pool if the drapes are open and where Lovejoy napped so often while I swam laps during his last few months.

"Hubert has a heart for church work," Dave said, settling back. I fought the urge to offer them wine and said, "Iced tea?" instead.

As if they had agreed beforehand not to accept refreshments, Dave answered without consulting Hubert: "We have other stops to make, but we just wanted to swing by and see how you are holding up."

"I'm holding up," I replied.

Hubert nodded, nodded, as if he understood, and I gave him a version of Lovejoy's smile that I sometimes felt on my face. I hadn't expected that to happen, but my husband had bequeathed to me some of his priceless smiles.

The smile triggered something in Hubert. He jumped into the conversation. "No one expected Mr. Frank to marry you four years ago when he was supposed to talk with you about missions."

Dave shook his head quickly, but Hubert didn't see him. He saw only Lovejoy's smile on my face. "But then it turned out to be a true love story for sure, but that was a surprise. A happy ending all around."

Nothing happened to me with that announcement. No cold pall settled into my chest. No acerbic remark flew out of my mouth. I just nodded easily and smiled, somewhat distantly now.

"I know," I said, finally to Dave. Some part of me had always known. That first day when Lovejoy had asked me to lunch, he had been sent to solve the problem assigned to him: me and the loveless ways I talked at church.

He had solved the problem by loving me.

Fearing that Hubert's words would cost me a night's sleep later, Dave leaned forward and said, "I'm not breaking confidentiality now if I tell you that Frank told me himself how much he loved you. He said you were special."

"Special," I replied. I met his gaze squarely, and sensing that he had said something he shouldn't have but didn't know what exactly, Hubert grew uncomfortably quiet.

"Are you okay?" Dave asked.

"Of course," I said.

"And you don't need anything from the deacons because they stand ready to fill in the gap—to help with whatever you need. That's what they're here for. To help widows and orphans."

I had been managing for the past seven months on my own. Just because Lovejoy was alive didn't mean he had been helping with anything. But now that he was formally gone, the deacons stood ready to help.

The offer made me feel tired. Very tired.

I didn't want to draw either of the two men in my living room, and after they made their good-byes and left, headed to their next stop, I decided I was finished with drawing. For a while anyway.

That surprised me because a fierce passion for it had come upon me with Lovejoy. I had pictures of him all over the house in various stages of repose, but ultimately, my sketches of him changing were no more telling than the photographs of that old house that the professional shutterbug took to capture the story of a building winding down, fading over time—with time because of the unrelenting sunlight. Neither my drawings of Lovejoy nor those photographs of an aging gothic house could capture and tell what we were both trying to say—to preserve. The story of life inside a house or with a man can only be kept inside the person who lives there. And I lived with Lovejoy. Was born again. Died with him in a way I didn't know existed. I gave up my house, I gave up my money, I gave up the idea of me for his idea of me, and I learned to love myself and everyone I met with greater generosity.

Although he had given away about a third of my money, after he was gone, I still had enough money to drink iced tea with every meal I bought in restaurants. You think that's not a big deal—to spend money on yourself in the name of tender mercies, but it is. Treating yourself to iced tea helps you to become more generous with others; and after Lovejoy, I was kinder and more generous with the people he would have recognized as people who needed tender mercy.

Each Christmas I sent Marjeen and her son a check. The boy is growing up in the church with me and the women who study him and cast sidelong glances at me. The boy does look like his grandfather, but I don't explain that to anyone. What is there to say? Marjeen and the boy were his responsibility, and now for Lovejoy's sake, I keep an eye on them. We all need somebody to love, don't we?

And I keep an eye on beauty and take it home with me whenever I can. I no longer walk past magnolia trees or if I go with a friend to harvest flowers for tabletop centerpieces, I always take some flowers home with me to put in small saucers around the house admiring their beauty and their scent. After a while when I have enjoyed them for a measure of time, I take them to the graves of Lovejoy, Amanda, and Darla and sprinkle the petals on top of them all.

It took six months for his gravestone to arrive, but when it did the words engraved on the granite told the truth about Frank and how I loved him. Each carved letter cost five glasses of iced tea. "His life was a love song."

I know. I was married to Frank Lovejoy for four and a half years. I believed everything he told me, and I loved him.

Visit from a Cereal Killer….

Retired school teacher Mildred Budge was standing naked in her laundry room remembering how her friend Cleo had died in the same state of undress, when she heard her front doorbell ring the first time. It couldn't be anyone she knew. All of Mildred Budge's friends knew to use the back door by the kitchen.

The timing was bad.

Mildred thought maybe she would just let whoever had come to the wrong house go away, when the doorbell rang again. And then, again. Insistently.

There was no ignoring it.

Only Mildred was naked, and everything she had been wearing while tagging dusty, mite-ridden furniture in the hot attic was now rotating inside the washing machine. On top of the clothes dryer were three lone unmatched black socks and one set of long underwear: white cotton Cuddl Duds that Mildred had intended to put away until the following winter

As the bell rang five more times, Miss Budge decided that any clothes were better than none. Damp with perspiration and gritty with dust, she grabbed the Cuddl Duds and began the arduous task of wriggling into them. It wasn't easy. She looked down at herself in the clingy wintertime underwear that fit like a diaphanous white body stocking.

Victoria's Secret would not be hiring her pear-shaped frame to model lingerie.

"Miz Bulge! Are you all right in there?" A man's voice called out.

Her morning caller knew her, but she didn't recognize his voice. She heard the front doorknob jiggled impatiently. With a start, Miss Budge couldn't remember if she had locked the front door after bringing in the morning newspaper.

"I'm on my way!" Miss Budge called out, and her voice broke. Living alone with no one to talk to for long periods of time, one's voice became, occasionally, untrustworthy.

Tugging at the snug shirt that wanted to rise up and show her unpierced navel, Miss Budge hastily detoured to the foyer, pausing on the other side of her own front door to check the lock.

She peered through the peephole.

Miss Budge had never formally met her morning caller, but she did recognize him. Standing on her front door step was the young father who had moved with his wife and son into the old Garvin house across the street. The young man was wearing the same clothes she had always seen him in--faded black jeans and a black T-shirt. However, this was the first time the young father was close enough for Miss Budge to read the words stenciled on the front of the T-shirt: "Cereal Killer."

He was holding a large Ziploc bag with lumpy grains in it.

As she sent a news flash prayer to Jesus— 'There's a cereal killer at my front door and I'm not fully dressed'—she called out, "Another moment, dear boy! I'll be right with you."

Miss Budge scooted to her bedroom and hurriedly slipped into her thick white chenille robe that she had bought for $19 at an after-Christmas sale three months ago. Adrenaline pumping, she clumsily pushed her still naked feet into sage green plastic Crocs. They were the ugliest shoes she had ever seen, but astonishingly comfortable.

"Miz Bulge! Is everything okay in there?" The Cereal Killer pounded on the door this time. Three hard raps.

Miss Budge cinched the thick robe firmly around her waist and scurried back to the front door, the toe of her right Crocs catching on the rug. She stumbled, and her arms batted the air as she fought to keep her footing. She got her balance back as the doorknob rattled again noisily.

"You haven't fallen or something, have you?" he called through the door.

Miss Budge wrenched the cold brassy doorknob and swung the front door open.

"Of course, I have not fallen. Why would I?" Even as Miss Budge said the words, she remembered so many of her older friends for whom the end of their mobility was signaled by a commiserating tsk-tsk-tsk from every messenger who had ever delivered the dreaded news, "Oh, did you hear? She fell."

Cleo had fallen down naked in her laundry room and died alone. And she wasn't the only one of Mildred's acquaintances to begin that journey toward dependence on others in a hospital, nursing home, or assisted living with a fall.

Blinking at the mid-morning sunlight, Miss Budge offered a disciplined, cordial smile, one that had developed over twenty-five years of greeting scared fifth graders as a public-school teacher and which had not diminished in the past two years since her retirement. "Young man, what is it you require so urgently?"

"Miz Bulge?" The Cereal Killer confirmed, squinting downward to meet her brown-eyed gaze. "You're shorter than they said."

"Why would people discuss my height?" Miss Budge inquired immediately, meeting his gaze unwaveringly, though she had to look up to do so. Her neighbor was tall and lanky with the kind of loose posture and untoned muscles that indicates a dearth of exercise.

"No. They said you was a great teacher, and somehow I jess thought you would be taller," he finished lamely. "I'm Kenny from across the street," he announced with a tip of his head toward the old Garvin house. "We been meaning to come say hi. The wife sent this to you," Kenny declared, holding out a gallon-size plastic Ziploc bag of what appeared to be rolled oats with raisins and slivered almonds.

Miss Budge reached politely for the proffered bag. Gifts of food usually came in covered white paper plates or disposable tin pans that she and her friends from the Berean Sunday school class chose to use when taking food to someone's house.

Miss Budge held the cellophane bag of grains up to the foyer light as if it were a bottle of special wine whose color she wanted to check. "How thoughtful," she murmured. "Won't you come in, Kenneth?"

"Thank you, Miz Bulge," Kenny said, stepping into her foyer. A heavy silver key chain slapped against his leg. He patted it companionably as if it were a small pet that was keeping him company. Squared bluish-black marks that reminded Miss Budge of some ancient Celtic designs set off his otherwise unmarred youthful hands.

When she peered more closely Miss Budge saw that the cribbed symbols were not a mysterious message in need of decoding but a single letter tattooed on each knuckle across the back of his hand that ultimately spelled out: L-O-V-E. Although she did not understand the allure of what amounted to inking graffiti upon one's person, Miss Budge, a spinster Christian lady, did believe in love. She smiled beneficently, as she adjusted the beige rheostat light switch in her expansive foyer.

The overhead light grew brighter, illuminating the various black and white photos on the wall of southern bridges that she had collected at one time in her life. Miss Budge had once upon a time loved the sight of aged bridges—loved the lines and arcs and the hope of them, shores being connected so people could cross over. But that season in her life had passed. The pictures were still hung, now a memorial to her previous affection for them rather than a celebration of the old-timey bridges themselves.

Kenny blinked rapidly, confused. She saw that Kenneth's eyes were a weak blue. Underneath the baseball cap that he did not take off, she assumed he was losing his hair prematurely.

"My last name is Budge. You have been calling me Miz Bulge," the retired teacher explained. She patted her mid-section. She was plumper than she had ever been. A frequent awareness of her increasing pear shape had not stopped the pounds from accruing, however. "But it's Mildred—Mildred Budge. Miss...." she declared forthrightly, unashamed of her singleness.

Kenny espied the pictures of solitary bridges on the walls. He blinked some more. The wispy, brown goatee on his chin waved gently when he spoke.

"Miz Deerborn told me about you."

"Will you sit down?" Miss Budge said, waving toward her living room. Her hands were bare of rings. She didn't wear jewelry when she had work to do, and she had spent a sticky morning in her hot attic tagging stored furniture that was to be taken and delivered to The Emporium, a local antique warehouse and flea market. She and her best friend Fran Applewhite were opening a sales booth.

Their initial inventory was the content of their respective attics: two lifetimes of acquired antiques (and a fair amount of old furniture) that would make them a fortune, predicted Fran--or at least enough money so they could travel some.

"I won't stay long," Kenny promised, stepping carefully as if he didn't want to leave footprints on the glossy wooden floor. Kenneth's navy and white athletic shoes made the same small sticking sound against the taffy-colored hardwood floor as her green Crocs. As if mesmerized, her visitor revolved slowly, taking in the room before sitting down on the yellow chintz sofa and saying with wonder, "It's so clean in here."

Miss Budge automatically surveyed her living room, pausing to twist the clear plastic prismatic rod that opened her front mini-blinds. The room filled with sunlight. As the room grew brighter, Miss Budge saw that she needed to dust again. There was a small scrap of clipped white paper which must have escaped her paper shredder resting on the border of the large red and blue oriental carpet that defined the floor space. In a culture that necessarily lived with the threat of identity theft, Miss Budge had become a dedicated shredder of her monthly bills on which the numbers, if obtained, could facilitate the stealing of her credit cards, bank accounts, and most importantly, her identity. While shredding was yet another routine chore, Miss Budge liked doing it. She had invested in a sturdy stand-alone monster shredder from Costco that was stationed next to the telephone table, a superior style of furniture made sadly obsolete by cell phones.

Itching to pick up that errant scrap of white paper that disturbed her sense of order, Miss Budge said instead, "Kenneth, are you thirsty?" She had not lost that school teacherly tone. "Do you want a drink?" Her head bobbed up and down encouragingly. When she did, her brown curls caught the light, creating a halo effect that she would have enjoyed if she had known it was happening. She didn't.

"It's too early for me," Kenny said, sitting back on the sofa. "But you go ahead and take a drink if you need a little something. I know how it is. I've got a granny who likes her wine in the morning, too."

Miss Budge's spine lengthened as her posture aligned itself with the truth.

"I do not need something to drink," she said, taken aback. Her forehead furrowed, deepening the lines that had grown from squinting while grading endless stacks of compositions written by students who did not have good penmanship. Miss Budge absentmindedly massaged the tender place between her eyebrows that felt now like it retained some perpetual nerve damage. Then, she pressed her brown plastic eye glasses up on her nose; they slipped periodically. Soon, it would be time to go see Mr. Cates. He had been keeping her glasses adjusted for thirty years.

"Me and my wife moved in to that old house two months ago," Kenny said, with a jut of his whiskery chin toward the old Garvin house across the street.

Since Ron Garvin had died of some kind of dementia the legality of his last will had been questioned, and the potential heirs were fighting over his estate. The Garvin house was being rented out by the executor until the domicile could be legally sold and the profits distributed

"Linda didn't want to live in Old Geezerville," Kenny explained, apparently unaware that the castigation of the Garden District in Montgomery, Alabama as Old Geezerville might be insulting to someone who had lived there her whole life.

The old geezers in reference were the long-time citizens of a southern city that had not only been the birthplace of the civil rights movement, but was also the home place of Zelda Fitzgerald, a famous belle and the wife of F. Scott. For those who cared, country singer Hank Williams was buried over at Oakwood Cemetery not too far from where Nathaniel Coles had lived when he was four years old with his family. In his teens he dropped the "s" and became Nat King Cole.

"I finally talked Baby into it. Our house is awesome. Really awesome, you know. We have what they call an attic fan. You can turn it on and open the windows. The air comes through just like the air conditioner was on," Kenny bragged. "It's going to save us a ton of money this summer, and it's already getting hotter by the day.

We believe in going green." Kenny stared out at his own home through Miss Budge's front window and took a deep breath.

"Me and the wife make organic cereal. That's what I brought you right there. It'll get you going regular. That's our sales hook. These days, you either sell to people who can't sleep, can't lose weight, or to people who can't...." Kenny struggled for the word he needed, pressing his thin lips together, and finally settled on, "Who can't *go*. Cereal can't help you sleep," Kenny added lamely. "Although if that's all you ate, you probably could lose some weight."

There was an awkward pause.

Miss Budge could not discern Kenny's real purpose in coming to see her. Had he caught a glimpse of her and decided she needed to go on a diet?

Miss Budge was an unabashed size-14 woman, but fleshing out the seams of one's garments seemed to happen inevitably as one grew older. The better part of wisdom was to practice moderation in eating, walk as much as you could, and then accept your anatomy as it developed.

Miss Budge eyed the Cereal Killer with curiosity. It seemed unlikely to her that any newcomer would make it his personal mission to infiltrate an older neighborhood and then call on the plumper residents with the goal of putting them on a cereal diet in order to sell his product. Still, she could not recall a time in her life when anyone other than the doctor had ever brought up the subject of her regularity. She decided that the prudent course would be to change the subject.

"I know you are new to the neighborhood. It is actually referred to as Cloverdale—to some, Old Cloverdale," the retired school teacher explained patiently. When Kenny blinked as if he didn't speak English, she explained, "Cloverdale is considered to be the heart of historic Montgomery."

Lovejoy

Kenny blinked some more, as if he didn't recognize the name of the city where they lived. Miss Budge smiled encouragingly, and continued politely. "I wonder if you have visited the Fitzgerald museum yet? It is to your left, about two miles that way," Miss Budge directed, pointing, and one more time, saw her mother's hand. She did not mind the vision of her mother's hand extending from her arm at all. Though no one expected a woman of Miss Budge's age to miss a parent, Mildred Budge still did miss her mother and was glad for the company of even the image of her mother's hand.

Kenny eyed the older woman as if she were speaking a foreign language. His eyes morphed to a weak shade of green. Miss Budge wondered if Kenneth was weak or just young. She had taught many young people and had learned that looking into their eyes and making assessments about intelligence or character based on an expression or shade of eye color had very little to do with who they really were—no more than how people once used to feel the bumps on a person's cranium to determine intelligence. Knowing that (and it had taken her a surprisingly long time to learn it) Miss Budge often fought the impulse anyway to know a person's head shape with her fingertips, like a blind person might. Kenny had a rectangular-shaped head. Her fingers began to strum the air gently. If she could know the contours of his head with her hands, what would the arcs and bumps tell her about what was going on inside? She clasped her hands determinedly in her lap and held them there while surreptitiously checking the closure of her robe.

Her mother would have liked this robe, too, she thought—and smiled.

"The museum is the old house of a famous Montgomery family. F. Scott Fitzgerald is a famous author. He married a Montgomery girl," she explained patiently. "You may recall from your high school days that Fitzgerald wrote *The Great Gatsby*."

Kenny stared at Miss Budge blankly, and the color of his eyes deepened to the color of an ocean just before it rained. Troubled, Kenny tried to figure out what to say next.

When he didn't immediately speak, Miss Budge continued. "His wife Zelda Sayre was not only a famous southern belle here but a talented writer as well."

Kenny's fingertips scratched the tops of his thighs as if he were getting ready to explain the purpose of his visit. Miss Budge nodded encouragingly, but Kenny did not respond to her cue.

"Or, there's Martin Luther King, Jr.'s church downtown or The First White House of the Confederacy," she added, sounding like one of those volunteer tour guides that some senior citizens become to fill their days after they retired. Though she was retired— prematurely, according to some—she was still too busy to volunteer in that capacity.

Kenny blinked and said, "Awesome." He rubbed his palms on the tops of his jeans. The silver chain with the keys jangled. He petted it.

Miss Budge felt impatient then, though she hid it. Fran and Winston were coming over with the truck in a half hour, and she needed to shower and dress before they arrived. Certainly, the delivery of cereal could not have been Kenneth's primary goal. "Are you sure you don't want some lemonade?" his hostess prompted. She could get it, he could drink it, he could leave.

Kenny shook his head, no, looking as if he might rise. But he didn't. "Miz Bulge...."

Determined to be polite, Miss Budge sat back in the uncomfortable turquoise chair. She had forgotten how unforgiving the chair was. Miss Budge shifted her derriere, struggling for a different center of gravity that might ease the rigidity, but she did not find it.

"Miz Bulge," Kenny said, beginning again, his gaze drifting around the room. "I been watching your house, and you go to church on Sundays. You carry a Bible and everything," Kenny declared. And his nervous hands came to a rest on the tops of his thighs, as he looked to his right at the table with the reading lamp. There were three different Bibles on it.

Kenny's eyes caught hers, and he pressed on. "My son is not a friendly boy. It's like he's not even there sometimes, you know? He's seven. He's supposed to be in school; but Baby---Linda, my wife---thinks Chase won't fit in at school because of his not talking. She's been trying to home school him, but it ain't going as well as she hoped it would. Baby's not a teacher, don't you see?" Kenny said, and his tattooed fingers began to strum the tops of his black-denimed thighs again, spelling out L-O-V-E over and over again.

Miss Budge nodded almost imperceptibly, and the warmth in her brown eyes faded to a wary watchfulness.

"You being a schoolteacher and all..."

Mildred assumed the 'and all' referred to going to church on Sunday and carrying a Bible.

"And I hear you still go to houses of sick kids sometimes...."

"Not anymore," Mildred replied carefully. Initially, after her sudden decision to retire two years ago--and because she needed the money to supplement her reduced fixed income--Miss Budge had accepted short-term assignments as a teacher for homebound students.

But she hadn't done that work for long. The children were too sick and too brave, and they had asked Miss Budge questions that were too hard to answer. She knew the answers; she just didn't want to say them out loud to young children in pain.

Kenny slapped the tops of his black jeans and finally got to his point. "I was wondering if you could help my boy."

"I am not a doctor," Mildred Budge replied, postponing the polite but firm 'no' she would offer Kenny in a moment just as soon as she framed it in her mind. She had left that kind of work behind--cried as many tears as she could. Besides, it was never wise to get caught up in the neighbors' domestic problems, especially if they lived as close as across the street. Before she could say no, her telephone rang.

Loudly.

Miss Budge had only one phone, and she kept the ringer on 'Loud' so that she could hear it ring anywhere in the house. She always answered her phone calls beside her wooden telephone table where a writing tablet and pen were readily available for note-taking and where the small seat built into the table gave her a place to rest in case the caller was long-winded. She sat there to do her monthly shredding, too. Other people thought that speaking on the telephone or shredding the monthly bills were tasks that happened in concert with other activities; it was called multitasking. But Mildred Budge did not like splitting her attention; she liked being focused, had learned as a school teacher that giving one's attention to a person or a job resulted in a better understanding of that person and a better job when work was to be done.

Kenny waited for Miss Budge to move and answer the telephone. She did not.

"I don't answer the telephone when I have a guest," Miss Budge explained simply as the ringing continued, then stopped abruptly.

Kenny laughed. Genuinely. As if the explanation of good manners was some kind of joke. "Miz Deerborn said you was funny and for me not to be afraid of you."

Ah, Belle Deerborn. The well-intentioned woman—and a good friend, too-- who lived just behind Mildred Budge on the other side of the circle that connected their intersecting yards.

Kenneth leaned forward and said in what was almost a whisper: "Miz Belle said you have the gift of healing kids."

Immediately, Miss Budge began to shake her head, no. "I was a teacher. That is all," she replied firmly. "You are wrong—and so is Belle—if you think otherwise."

"Miz Deerborn said you would say that," Kenny replied immediately, his brown wispy goatee wagging.

"It is the truth," Miss Budge replied unswervingly. "I do not glamorize the fruits of determined work by calling it something it is not."

Kenneth nodded as if he were in on the conspiracy of discretion that Miss Budge was determined to perpetuate. "Maybe you could jess speak to my boy then," he said with a wink. "Jest your speaking to him would be good, 'cause Chase don't talk to nobody, even us, sometimes." Kenny took an anxious breath and switched tactics, attempting to persuade her. "That cereal I brought you is all organic. 'S very good for you. No chemicals, pesticides, etcetera, etcetera, etcetera. Let me know if you like it, and I'll bring you a bunch more." Kenny stood up then suddenly. He had finished the job he had given himself to do. The sun shifted from behind a cloud and spilled fresh illumination into the room right where he was standing. The angles of his square-shaped head were easily discerned as bumps inside the baseball cap which he had never removed. Miss Budge read his mind then: he had come to see the lady across the street, brought her his offering, made his request, and now he was going home.

Miss Budge was ready for him to go, and she stood more slowly, not because she was older or creaky or less able to stand, but because in her generation one did not rush others out the door by rising too quickly. There was always a hint in every gesture that parting was sweet sorrow—really.

Miss Budge smiled as she followed him to the foyer, speaking in the pace of having an infinite amount of time to get to know other people that others erroneously and inappropriately judged harshly as an irritating habit of an older person, but it was only courtesy.

DAPHNE SIMPKINS

"That explains why the UPS truck comes to your house so often. He must be bringing you supplies for your organic cereals," she theorized aloud, as Kenny led the way to her front door.

Kenny's voice grew proud. "We sell on the internet a lot, and we take it over to the health food store on the Easter by-pass. We have mucho customers now," Kenny said proudly, as her telephone began to ring again. "Somebody really wants to talk to you," Kenny said. "I'll go on and get out of your way."

He turned in the doorway and said, his voice growing quieter: "My boy's name is Chase, and you don't know him yet, but he's special."

Miss Budge met the young father's gaze, so similar to the faces of so many young parents of young children who had been in her care during the twenty-five years she had served the state in the public-school system. Kenny was a stranger, but Miss Budge knew him. Kenny was a young father who had a son who was special.

"You could come over any time. Any time at all that suits you. Linda would love to meet you," Kenny promised, looking across the street to his new home where the blinds were closed, and no lights appeared to be on inside. There was something in that anxious glance at his own home that moved Miss Budge. She relented.

"I'd be delighted to meet your Chase," Mildred agreed, casting an involuntary glance at the insistent telephone as it continued to ring.

Kenneth fired an imaginary pistol at her with his forefinger and thumb, and Miss Budge marveled at a hand gesture that spoke of a violence that was inconsonant with the nature of his request. Still, she fought the urge born of politeness to mimic Kenneth's hand movement, offering a short wave of farewell instead as she walked toward the telephone. On the way, Mildred stooped over and picked up the scrap of white paper that had been bothering her. It was a piece of notebook paper, not a piece of a shredded bill.

"Greetings to you and yours," Miss Budge said, answering the phone.

"Have you been drinking?" Fran Applewhite asked sharply.

Before Mildred could answer, Fran said, "That was me calling before; but then I thought you might be in the attic, and if I let it keep ringing, you might break your neck trying to answer the telephone. You don't want to die in the attic. It would have been hard as all get-out to bring your body down those stairs. Remember how hard it was to get the broken water heater down? So, I hung up and waited a spell. I have news. It's big," Fran warned.

"I was not in the attic. I was in my living room talking with a cereal killer who thinks that the Eastern by-pass is named after Easter Sunday or the Easter bunny. It is unclear which one he has in mind."

Fran interrupted her. "Mildred, she's killed another one."

Mildred didn't have to ask who Fran meant. She knew. Liz Luckie had recently married for the fourth time; and each time, the husbands had died early in the marriage. Mildred had not known the first three husbands, but she had been a special friend of Liz's most recent groom.

"How did Hugh die?" Mildred asked. She sat down heavily in the small seat built into the telephone table. It was a tight fit. It didn't use to be.

"The regular way. Natural causes." Fran reported bluntly.

"Natural causes. Again," Mildred repeated bleakly. She patted her face with one hand. She felt pale. Then, she pressed the same hand to her chest. Her heart was beating fast. The chenille robe was thick. She was wearing long underwear, too, but Mildred felt chilled. Her lower lip trembled. No hot flash conveniently arrived when it might have helped to warm her.

"They all die of natural causes," Fran said quietly. She hesitated before adding, "Today's Thursday. I figure the funeral will be Saturday."

Mildred nodded into the telephone, her throat instantly dry. Yes. That might be hard for someone else to arrange, but for a woman who had already orchestrated three funerals for her previous husbands, arranging a funeral in two days would not be a problem. She wouldn't have the funeral on a Sunday afternoon, and Monday was too late.

"I wanted to tell you before Winston and I got there together with his truck because that's not the kind of news you need to hear in front of company," Fran explained, her voice dropping to a whisper.

Winston must have come inside Fran's house and was now standing near enough to Fran to hear what she was trying to tell Mildred quietly.

Mildred swallowed hard, remembering how before Hugh had married Liz, his fingertips had grazed hers in the church kitchen when he had handed her his water glass to be washed on a Saturday morning. Each had volunteered to participate in the deep spring cleaning of the church building.

And before that, Hugh had sat beside her in Sunday school as if he just happened to land there and how nervous his sitting close had made her feel—and crowded.

And Hugh had asked her to dance after one of the church weddings at the country club, and she hadn't said no fast enough. Hugh had taken her in his arms and steered her around, and while they moved—scuttled crablike is how Mildred described it to herself—about the floor, she had endured an embarrassing hot flash and broken out in a flop sweat of sorts that Hugh didn't seem to notice, but, of course, he had noticed.

"I've got to go now, Millie. It'll be all right," Fran whispered before hanging up. Mildred's best friend said the words with the authority of a veteran widow who had told herself the same thing through many a long night spent without Gritz who had died on her—the husband Fran Applewhite had loved dearly for forty-three years.

BOOKS BY DAPHNE SIMPKINS

Belle—a Mildred Budge Friendship story—The first novel in a spin-off series that focuses on Belle who lives across the field from Mildred Budge

What Makes a Man a Hero? Stories about Men for Father's Day

Miss Budge Goes to Fountain City—A story about running away from Christmas only to find it in the city across the river

The Bride's Room—The third full-length novel in the Mildred Budge series about love and marriage and friendship

Blessed A touching collection of inspiring stories about loving others well throughout your life with all the labels associated with mothering, fathering, daughtering, and caregiving.

The Mission of Mildred Budge The second collection of short stories about church life in the South featuring Mildred Budge and friends.

Christmas in Fountain City A heartwarming story about neighborhoods and neighboring at Christmastime and throughout the year.

What Al Left Behind—Essays that are helping to rewrite the social narrative that the effect of dementia and Alzheimer's is only a meaningless tragedy. It isn't. These essays point readers toward meaning and hope.

A Cookbook for Katie—A memoir masquerading as a cookbook with recipes and reveries for the bride written by an aunt to her niece.

Mildred Budge in Embankment—This second novel in four books featuring Mildred Budge and friends focuses on a pulpit committee trying to find the right preacher for their old-fashioned but growing Southern church.

Mildred Budge in Cloverdale—This is the first full-length novel in the Mildred Budge books.

Miss Budge in Love—This first collection of short stories features Mildred Budge and friends.

The Long Good Night—A memoir about growing up in the South while taking care of her father who was living out his days with dementia.

Nat King Cole: A Life of Music—A biography for children about the famous crooner who was born in Alabama.

ABOUT DAPHNE SIMPKINS

Daphne Simpkins is an Alabama writer who lives in her hometown of Montgomery, Alabama. She writes on a variety of subjects that include Nat King Cole, cooking, caregiving, church life in the South, and a series of books about Southern church lady and retired school teacher Mildred Budge. Befriend her on Facebook, Twitter, or Linkedin.com. To keep up with her book news, follow her on Amazon, BookBub, and Goodreads.